Inherit The Tides
Summer Adrift

E V McMillan

Color Your World Press, 2024

Betty Smith, the author of A Tree Grows in Brooklyn,
was once quoted as saying,
"The world was hers for the reading,"

However, I must add that
"The magic was mine for the writing."
~E V McMillan

For my family, my friends, and every reader who turned
these pages—your belief made this possible.

Also By E V McMillan

The Summer Adrift Series:
Shifting Tides
Wild Tides
Inherit the Tides

Author's Note

Thank you for picking up Inherit the Tides, the third and final installment of The Summer Adrift Series. It's been a long and incredible journey, and I'm grateful you've been a part of it. Writing this book, like the series itself, has been more than just putting words on a page—it's been an exploration of growth, resilience, and the power of finding one's place in the world.

This story, like many, reflects not only the characters and their adventures but also the journey of the writer behind it. It's about facing fears, embracing change, and honoring those who have shaped us along the way. It's a reminder that the path we take is never straightforward, but it's in the twists and turns that we discover who we truly are.

As you've followed Quinn, Jordan, and the rest of the crew through their triumphs and challenges, I hope you've found a piece of your own journey reflected in theirs. Thank you for joining me on this adventure, for cheering on these characters, and for making this series what it is. Your support and enthusiasm mean everything. Here's to the waves we ride, the dreams we chase, and the stories that shape us.

With gratitude,
E V McMillan

CHAPTER
ONE

Biarritz, France
Four months earlier…

The morning sun was beginning to claw its way above the horizon, tearing through the remnants of night with streaks of gold and pink.

The heat, unseasonably intense for May, already pressed down like a heavy hand, promising another stifling day. I walked away from the beach, the familiar rumble of the ocean fading as I headed up the cliff-side road. The scent of salt air mingled with the sweet perfume of blooming jasmine and lavender, an intoxicating blend that would have been soothing if not for the strange tension in the air. It felt like the calm before a storm—a quiet unease I couldn't shake as I moved through the waking town. The town was waking up, the soft chatter of early risers blending with the clinking of dishes from nearby cafes. But my mind was elsewhere. The heat, the crowds—it all felt too much, too soon. We'd been on vacation for nearly two weeks, but the restless energy still buzzed in my veins. I couldn't shake the feeling that something was off. Maybe it was just the pressure of being here, competing again, or maybe it was something deeper, something I couldn't quite put my finger on.

I passed by the quaint shops and cafes lining the promenade, their doors just beginning to open for the day. The scent of fresh coffee drifted out, mingling with the ocean air, a familiar comfort. The houses here, with their red and white facades, looked like they'd been plucked from a postcard, standing in contrast to the sleek modern villas that dotted the cliffs. It was hard to believe this quiet town would soon be buzzing with life, the peaceful streets flooded with surfers, tourists, and fans. But for now, there was a stillness I wished I could hold onto.

As I made my way back to the hotel, the sun climbed higher, burning away the last traces of the marine layer. The streets were coming to life, but the tension in my chest only grew. I kept checking my phone, expecting—what? A message? A warning? I didn't know. But when Lloyd's phone buzzed, followed by a chorus of pings from the rest of our group, I knew it wasn't good. We all did.

This was my third time in Biarritz, but my second time competing in the International Tourney. Colin, our coach and mentor, had prepared the five of us—his guppies on the team—that we would unlikely walk away with any honors in our division. Still, it was one of the best training grounds to hone our skills. None of us had advanced beyond the second-level elimination heats, but we celebrated nonetheless and with great enthusiasm. Today was the last day. We would watch from the sidelines as Josh, our team captain, prevailed.

All afternoon yesterday, Josh had battled waves that seemed to encapsulate the spirit of the Tourney. Raging swells pushed the ten competitors to their limits, each ride a breathtaking display of skill and determination. The heats had ended with Josh a fraction of a point behind the reigning three-time champion, Piper Lewis. If he continued today as he did yesterday, he could dethrone Lewis and claim the title of Ultimate Surfer.

Taking a deep breath, feeling a smile tug at the corners of my mouth, I started back down the road toward the beach and the hotel, where my teammates—my family—were likely waking up and getting ready for the day. While most of the team would soon be packing up and scattering to points unknown, my mates and I would be moving just a half kilometer away to a small villa we'd rented for the next month. Villa Coeur de la Mer, or Heart of the Sea, sat right on the ocean's edge, self-sufficient and secluded. We were all looking forward to a few weeks of nothing but surf, sand, and sun.

We'd only been on vacation for nearly two weeks, and we'd already burned through every activity on our month-long bucket list. Jordan Smith, Grayson Pierce, Joey Maldonado, Lloyd Carter, and I made the most of every day and night. We surfed, para-glided, hiked, mountain-biked, caught a few rugby matches, and even attempted golf—though not very well. One day, we took a trip to Bayonne to soak in some history. Every evening, we'd return to the Villa, shower, change, and head back out to dive into the nightlife, meeting beautiful locals and tourists alike. I doubt I've ever felt so carefree or enjoyed myself so much.

After more than a week of non-stop activity, it didn't take much convincing for us to spend one evening at the Villa, chopping it up around the huge stone fireplace with a snapping, crackling fire. The warmth wrapped the large common room in a comforting embrace, keeping out the unseasonable chill of the light, drizzly rain that had descended on the town. And though we still had another two weeks left, we were already starting to look forward to getting back on the water and reuniting with the rest of the team. We were expected to meet up with everyone in Peniche, Portugal. Josh, Sean, and Colin would have cut their vacation short so that Josh could fly out to Jo'berg to deal with sponsors and Colin could spend some time in New South Wales with his family. Sean and Jeff would no doubt make a detour to conquer the Banzai Pipeline in Oahu—again—before meeting us in Peniche. Marc and Vince were on the East Coast, in North Carolina and Florida, respectively, spending time with family. Strangely enough, I missed them all. A month was the longest we'd all been apart in the three years I'd been with the team, the first real vacation any of us had in all that time, but I, for one, was looking forward to us getting back together.

Sated from a heavy dinner of meat and pasta with a thick cheese sauce that was now my new favorite, fresh-baked bread, and drinks, we'd kicked back in companionable silence. Someone was streaming American pop music on their phone when, suddenly, our phones began pinging. While it normally wasn't cause for alarm—most of us had alerts set to notify us whenever anything about our team or team members was mentioned on social media—it was unusual for so many alerts to go off at once. Lloyd was the first to open his news feed to breaking news. He drew a horrified breath and showed us several grainy photos of a surfer lying in the sand, a tourniquet wrapped around his leg, splashed up on the news app. He eerily looked like Josh. The caption read: *Joshua Alan Brenner, elite surfer and son of Australian billionaire James Brenner, titan and CEO of Brenner Industrials, attacked in a freak shark attack off the coast of San Diego.*

We quickly opened our phones and skimmed the plethora of articles, though most had scant details of the attack and his condition. We started calling and texting Josh, Colin, Sean—anyone and everyone we could think of, though our messages went straight to voicemail. We sat together for hours, reading every bit of news on the internet that we could find.

The next morning, as we debated packing up and finding flights to California, we got word from Jeff and Vince. Jeff confirmed that the accident was every bit as bad as reported, but there was nothing we could do in San Diego. He reassured us that Josh, though in critical condition, was expected to pull through, and Sean was fine. But he had no news on Colin. Immediately after, Vince called, telling us to sit tight—he and Marc were catching a flight to join us. It made no sense; we wanted to be in the States, not halfway across the globe. But we did as they asked, staying in the Villa, worrying, waiting. We figured it would take them at least fifteen hours to get from Paris to Biarritz.

The next evening, more than seventy-two hours after the first report of the accident, the heavy, sonorous sound of the doorbell echoed through the Villa, pulling us all down to the common room. Malcolm, the household manager—our steward, butler, valet, and housekeeper all rolled into one—was already greeting Vince and Marc when I made it downstairs. They had their gear with them, but they looked like they'd aged a decade. Their usual stoke was dialed down to zero. The whole vibe was off, so far off that I knew things had to be even worse than we'd imagined.

We pulled them into the common room while Malcolm handled their bags. The Villa had more than enough space for them to stay, and we were relieved to have them in charge. We dropped like stones onto the sofas and chairs, practically holding our breath. Silence filled the room like a thick fog as we stared at them, hoping the news wasn't as bad as what we'd conjured up in our heads. Vince, the elder guru of our crew—not just in years but in pure wisdom and surf soul—cleared his throat several times, struggling to drop the bomb on us.

"Guys, I'm sorry to have to bring this to you, but I need everyone to listen," he started, his usual chill replaced by a gnarly hesitation that wasn't his style. His words were heavy, like a big wave set on the horizon. My heart sank, catching this wave of dread.

"You know about the accident. Josh and Colin…" He barely got the words out, his voice low, and the room felt like it shrunk, the air thinning out. "Josh is in the hospital, hanging on but critical. The doctors expect him to pull through, but Colin…" Vince's voice broke, showing cracks we never saw. "Colin didn't make it."

Didn't make it? Those words were like a wipe-out, each one

a hit that knocked the wind out of me. Josh, our star, battling for his life? And Colin, the rock of our team, the guy who saw the spark in all of us, who pulled me into this world when I was just a grom fleeing from dark clouds—he didn't make it? That was unreal. Crazy. It couldn't be true.

What happened?" Lloyd demanded, his voice tight, while Joey echoed, "How could that happen?"

The questions we'd been holding back for the last seventy-two hours exploded, fast and furious, until Marc held up a hand.

"They were in SoCal. A freak shark attack went down. Josh suffered serious bites to his leg and thigh, and they think Colin… he never made it back to shore. They don't know what happened to him. The authorities presume he drowned. His body hasn't been recovered."

"From who? Who did you hear this from?" Jordan piped up, his voice a mix of shock and disbelief.

"Sean. He was there. The three of them were together."

My vision blurred, tears streaming down my face. My crew— we all felt it. Shock, sorrow, huddling together for the dude who was our north star and for Josh, whose light was flickering.

"How does something like this even happen? How does Colin just…drown?" My own voice was barely recognizable, shaky as I tried to make sense of it. Vince just shook his head.

"Details are sketchy, but Sean caught enough of it to lay it out for us."

"And Sean? He made it?" I asked, my throat tight.

"Yeah. He made it."

"So, what's our next move? Are we going to Cali?"

"No. We're going to hang tight. Marc and I came here to fill you in, and we're all gonna camp here till we get the full picture from Sean or Jeff. Sean's with Josh. Josh's family is flying in, and Jeff's taking point on the search and handling Colin's scene."

I nodded, tears falling into my lap. I don't know how long I sat there, lost in thought, staring at the space beside me where Colin would have sat, his laughter booming like rolling thunder, mercilessly teasing anyone and everyone. He had been more than a mentor to me—he was a father figure I'd craved, the guiding hand that had steered me away from the path of resentment and anger that my father and brother, a supportive brother and friend, had laid out. His belief in me was a stark contrast to the physical and mental abuse I'd escaped when I'd run away from home all those years ago. Losing him felt like being adrift at sea without a compass, a profound sense of disorientation. The grief that filled the room was a palpable force. Dark waters threatened to pull me under. The Villa, once a slice of paradise, now felt suffocating, as if the walls were closing in. I stood up and walked away, though it was an unconscious act. Vince's hand found my shoulder, a grounding force in the tumult of emotions, and I stopped and looked up.

"We're going to get through this, Quinn," he said, his voice firm despite the tremor of emotion. "Together. It's what Colin would have wanted and what Sean and Josh expect. We're a team, in and out of the water."

I think I nodded, and he turned back to continue answering the group's questions.

I needed space to think, to be alone, and I headed for the stairs to my room on the second floor. The pain I felt from Colin's loss was excruciating, made even more so because of how much I looked up to him. I didn't hear Jordan—my closest friend, my brother in every way that mattered—catch up with me at the foot of the stairs.

"You okay, Quinn?" he asked, putting a hand on my arm, his voice heavy with his own grief.

"I dunno. I can't believe it."

"I know. I can't either. Colin was an excellent swimmer. How could he just drown?"

I could hear the pain in his voice, that mix of disbelief and anger that I felt, too. I turned to clasp his shoulder, giving it a firm squeeze. Jordan and I were kindred spirits, though to look at us, you'd never know it. His deep caramel skin, sharp features, and thick dreadlocks pulled back in his usual way gave him a fierce, almost regal appearance. He carried the rich, vibrant energy of his Afro-Caribbean roots—roots that ran deep into a dirt-poor coastal village where every day was a struggle. Jordan's father fished the waters to keep food on the table while his mother taught in the local school, scraping by with barely enough to cover the basic needs of their eight kids.

For Jordan, surfing was more than a sport; it was a shot at a better life for his entire family. The ocean was his escape, his hope, the only place where he could be free from the weight of responsibility that had been on his shoulders since he was a kid. He rode waves like his life depended on it because, in so many ways, it did.

I came from a different world, but the struggles were familiar. Born and raised in Northern California, my family barely scraped by. My father was a stern, devout man who saw my passion for surfing as a distraction, something that needed to be beaten out of me. My older brother, Danny, was even worse—a bully who let his own failures fester into fists. When I finally left home, beaten and bruised, I had nothing but my board and the dream of making it on my own.

Meeting Colin, Josh, Sean, and the rest of the team was as clear as it had been yesterday. I'd been living on my own for a few months, and homelessness was a brutal education in adapting and surviving. I was hustling surfing matches on the beach so I'd have a few dollars every day to get something to eat. I'd mostly run out of challengers, having beaten most of the locals several times over. Then, this big guy showed up on the beach just when I'd considered moving on. He was clearly a vacationer but seemed to know his way around a surfboard. Anyway, we got to talking a little bit and I challenged him to a match. Yeah, I was cocky, but he wagered a hundred dollars that I couldn't beat him, and that kind of money was too good to pass up.

He won, of course, hands down. He was so far out of my league that he made me look like the amateur I was, but in a way, I also won. He saw something in me—spirit, determination, potential. Over the next couple of days, he and I talked about surfing, going pro and living the dream. He introduced me to the younger guys, Jordan, Gray, and Lloyd. The big dogs—Josh, Sean, Vince, Jeff and Marc were taking care of business in Venice Beach, a couple of hours away, and Joey hadn't joined up with them yet, but we all just clicked. So when they left the little town of Cypress Cove, I left with them.

You could say meeting Colin and the guys was fortuitous, but becoming one of them was life-changing. I felt like I'd found a part of me that had been missing. Family, camaraderie, purpose. Jordan and I both knew what it was like to feel out of place, to have something to prove. But more than that, we knew the value of loyalty, of having someone who got you, no questions asked.

Jordan gave me a nod, his face tight with emotions he was trying to keep under control. "He was like a brother to us, man. This isn't fair."

I nodded, swallowing the lump in my throat. "Yeah, it's not."

The weight of Colin's loss settled between us, heavy and suffocating, as we stood there in the quiet of our shared grief, shoulder to shoulder, letting the silence say everything we couldn't.

Days blurred together, one indistinguishable from the next. We rarely left the Villa, spending our time in the common room, the epicenter of our vigil. The television was constantly tuned to the news channels, muted, as we consumed every scrap of information about Josh or Colin like starving men. Yet with each passing day, the silence from the other side of the globe grew louder, a gaping void filled with our worst fears.

A few weeks ago, the Villa, with its sprawling rooms and

sunlit spaces, had been an idyllic retreat. The future had seemed as bright and limitless as the azure blue skies and turquoise ocean, and laughter had been our constant companion. Now, it felt as though the walls themselves mourned. The light was too harsh, the shadows too deep, and every sound too loud. We moved through the rooms like ghosts, our conversations a series of whispers and heavy silences. No one spoke of leaving, not even for food. The thought of missing a call or an update anchored us to the Villa with a weight heavier than grief. The outside world, with its relentless march forward, seemed a distant reality we were too willing to ignore. Our focus became singular—any news of Colin and any word on Josh's fight for life.

The blue gleaming pool went untouched, its sparkling waters a stark reminder of a joy we could no longer grasp. The tennis and pickleball courts and our surfboards were all ignored; the thought of hitting the waves without Colin's laughter or the anticipation of Josh's triumphant return felt like a betrayal.

In the early hours before dawn, I wandered to the balcony. Below, the ocean whispered promises of continuity, of waves that would keep coming long after we were gone. It was a comfort and a curse, a reminder of the impermanence of our troubles but also of the deep loss we had suffered.

Then, after more than a month of uncertainty and grief, Vince called us into a huddle. His voice, though heavy with the weight we all felt, was firm and decisive. "Time to get our heads back in the game," he said, locking eyes with each of us. "We've got waves to catch, for Josh, for Colin. They wouldn't want us bailing now. We need to honor them the best way we know how. Pack it up. We have a flight to catch."

His words were a beacon, cutting through the fog. We're surfers, heart and soul, with a lineup calling our names. The Villa, our refuge, had become a prison, a place where time stood still, and grief was our only companion.

That night, we began to gather our belongings because we were rolling out in the morning. Taghazout, Morocco, was our next stop on the league's itinerary, and we all felt like we were leaving a piece of ourselves behind. But the stoke slowly returned, mixed with grit, gratitude, and the drive to keep our legacy alive. Our job was far from over. Grief would accompany us, a noiseless specter that might never fully recede, but so too would the courage Colin taught us, the determination Josh exemplified in every competition, and the resilience we'd share in the days, weeks, and months ahead. As a team, our bond was solid—now forged in the hottest fires of loss and tempered in the deepest waters of brotherhood. We were ready, one and all, to do what we did best.

CHAPTER TWO

Southern California
September

We arrived at LAX in the early afternoon.

After navigating customs and baggage claim, I followed my mates outside to the coach bus boarding area. The heat and humidity hit us like a sauna, the air thick with the lingering dampness of earlier rain. Slinging my duffel over my shoulder, I tried to dodge the deepest puddles as I headed for our waiting bus.

Inside, I plopped down near the back, even though there was plenty of room for the eight of us. Vince, Jeff, and Marc were up front, locked in hushed conversation near the driver. Jordan, Joey, and Lloyd were in full chat mode in the middle, making terrible jokes and teasing each other. Gray stretched out across two seats across from me, pulling his baseball cap down over his eyes. Deciding to follow his lead, I leaned back and closed my eyes, hoping to catch some Zs. The bus lurched into motion, tossing us around like a rag doll before smoothing out on the road.

I was glad to be back in the States, especially in Huntington Beach. We usually only got to Southern California once a year, and this time, we were hoping to meet up with Sean and Josh for the first time since the accident four months ago. It would be good to see them again. Josh had had a helluva close call and was lucky to get away with his life. That shark went after him like he was a tasty treat, and he was in bad shape when Sean got him out of the water. Sean, along with Josh's family, had been solid in keeping us updated on Josh's recovery and rehab. He was also great at clarifying the truth buried in the media's crazy stories. For weeks, the internet had blown up with all the drone and cellphone footage, and the media circus that followed kept the story alive.

It still gutted me that Colin had never been found, but I was grateful that Sean had shared Colin's gear with us. Some of the guys used what they got, hoping it would bring them good karma in competitions, but for me, it was good karma just having some of it. Most of what I received was stored in a locker in Vista Valley, a town about ten miles from where my parents lived.

Despite the gravity of the situation, none of us bailed on the competitions. We pushed through the rest of the tour, winning and losing as a squad. We'd just wrapped up a rough two-week run. Ten days ago, we were shredding in Banyu Wangi, Indonesia, where we lost our shirts and our dignity. From there, we went directly to Playa Rincón in the Dominican Republic, and just yesterday, we finished a four-day meet in Teahupo'o, Tahiti. Last night, we drove a couple of hours to Papeete, Tahiti's capital city, to catch our midnight flight.

The rhythm of the bus on the highway was a lullaby, and I didn't realize I'd drifted off until Gray nudged me awake. We'd arrived at our crash pad, the Cielo De Mar Hotel. It was fancy, as always—five-star all the way. I shouldered my duffel and gear, followed everyone off the bus, and headed straight for the lobby. Snagging my room key, I heard a few of the guys buzzing about food and a night out. When they asked me to join, I passed. My plan was simple—a hot shower and a soft bed. I was ready to crash.

The next morning, feeling way more human, I walked into a lobby swarming with the who's who of the surf world—riders, reps, reporters. It was like stepping into a beehive of cameras and chatter, but I spotted the guys sitting in a restaurant on the lanai and joined them. I pulled up a chair between Joey and Gray.

"Get enough rest, Sleeping Beauty?" Gray teased.

"Of course. You know I need my beauty sleep."

"Well, maybe you need a few more hours," Joey smirked.

"Dude, no matter how much sleep you get, it doesn't seem to make a difference."

"That's because I can't get any prettier!"

We all laughed. Joey was an arrogant ass, but he was our arrogant ass. I flagged the server down and ordered a huge breakfast. It felt like my stomach was so empty my belly button was sticking to my spine.

"I got a text from Sean. He and Josh should be here around noon. They're driving up from San Diego," Jeff said.

"Do you think Sean's going to participate in the meet?" I asked.

"Haven't heard differently."

I nodded. Sean would bring in some needed cash. No one

would beat him now that Josh was out, and one check from him would likely top the money the rest of us would earn. Besides, it was always exciting watching him take on the waves. We chatted about random things until three servers came out carrying our food. I drowned my pancakes in strawberry syrup as soon as they were set down in front of me.

Later, we moved from the restaurant to the seating area on the other side of the lanai, chilling until we saw Sean pull up in a convertible, with Josh grinning from the passenger seat. Hotel staff swooped in to grab their gear and park the car. We all got up to greet them as they made their way to the lobby. I locked on Josh, trying to get a read on him, checking to see if anything was different. He was moving a bit gingerly on his left side, but man, he looked good—tanned and way stronger than I'd expected. Seeing him standing tall and unbroken, greeting us with a touch and a handshake, lifted a huge weight off my shoulders. He looked solid, and I was relieved to see him like that.

I followed them inside, feeling the stoke coming off everyone as people recognized them. The energy in the room spiked as people crowded around, dozens of voices becoming an excited roar. Josh was the main attraction, Sean moving aside so the team and everyone else could get his attention. He was all smiles, high-fives, and bro-hugs, even though you could tell he'd probably kill for a chance to give his leg a rest. I mentally nodded at his cool handling of the mob. He was a natural with people—outgoing and charismatic, never ignoring or turning anyone away. I saw Sean move out of the limelight, noting how chill he was compared to Josh. They were like brothers, but night and day. Sean was always in the background, running things, keeping everything moving like a well-oiled machine. He seldom mugged for the shutter-hounds, though they probably followed him as much as they did Josh. Our brand was as tight as a bank vault because of how Sean handled things. He wasn't the kind to make rash decisions.

Vince, Marc, and Jeff joined Sean on the sidelines, keeping one eye on Josh. I guess the three of them were Josh's de facto bodyguards, always ready to push back the crowd when it got too tight. They seemed content enough to chat on the sidelines. I cut through the crowd and went to stand beside Sean, who flipped around, all smiles, and hit me with a firm clasp on the shoulder.

"How's it going, Quinn?"

"Keeping it together, Sean. How about you?"

"Good, good. You alright?" He asked after my well-being in a way that went beyond the moment. I nodded.

"Yeah, I'm okay. Thanks for sending me Colin's gear. I don't know how to tell you how much that meant to me."

"I already know, Quinn. You guys were like little brothers to him. You were as important to him as he was to you."

"Still, I just appreciate you looking out."

"Of course, man. You all checked in?" I nodded again, and he squeezed my shoulder. Turning back to Jeff and Vince, he said, "I'm ready to get some grub. How about we meet in twenty?"

"Yeah, sounds good. The Dolphin Room?" Vince asked.

They'd apparently been making plans before I showed up. Sean nodded and glanced over at Josh. The dude looked pretty wiped despite the big grin on his face, and Marc broke off from us to disperse the crowd.

"Heads up, everyone," Jeff shouted, his voice carrying across the lobby. "We're rallying in the Dolphin Room in twenty for some grub and a huddle, yeah? Josh and Sean need to shoot up to their rooms before they meet us there. Any questions, see Vince."

Sean pat me on the back again and moved away, heading toward the bank of elevators. Vince and I watched Marc break up the crowd around Josh so he could disentangle himself from the well-wishers and head for the elevators. With a big grin on his face, Vince grabbed me in a one-armed headlock, squeezing me against his side and laughing raucously. Jeff, seeing me helpless, came over and jabbed me twice—once in the bicep, then in the side—while Vince kept me locked in his armpit. I was apparently their punching bag for the afternoon.

"I was keen on just sipping my lunch, but I guess I could munch on something too," Jeff said, finally stepping back, though he gave me another jab to the ribs. Vince shot a look from him to me and shrugged. Without a word, he released me and bailed, likely heading to the Dolphin Room, leaving me disheveled and none too steady. Jeff followed him, flexing his biceps and laughing loudly.

The Dolphin Room was a small private dining and conference room with large windows overlooking a long stretch of ocean and sandy beach. The heavy blackout drapes were pulled aside, letting in bright afternoon sunlight. Lunch was an assortment of sandwiches and cold salads, which we scarfed down quickly while listening to Josh and Sean share everything they'd been through over the last few months. We even got a chance to tease Josh for falling in love with the doctor who'd saved him. Though we teased him, we were massively happy for him.

When the food was cleared away, Jordan picked up his glass and tapped it to get everyone's attention. The room fell silent as we turned to him, my anxiety bubbling up because I knew what was coming next.

"So, check this," he said, his dark brown eyes flashing. "Quinn and I have been thinking… what if we hit the waves for a paddle-out tonight?" It was more of a statement than a question. "We know Colin's folks had a private service for him back in Australia, but most of us missed out. Doing it together would be solid—for the team."

Silence settled over the table as everyone weighed the idea. I caught a glimpse of Josh's face tensing up, then smoothing over just as quickly.

"Can we get enough flower leis in such a short time?" Sean asked, sounding like he might be in.

"We can probably get enough for us, but we'll see how many extras we can get," Jordan said quickly. "Tonight's the only shot we've got. With tomorrow being go-time, from sunup to sundown, there won't be another chance. It won't matter if it's just us. He was our bro, our rock."

"And what's the play? Keep it just us, or open it up to who-ever's down for it?" Marc asked.

I smiled, feeling my anxiety start to fade. "Anyone…every-one is welcome. I'm sure a few people will want to come and honor him."

"The more, the merrier," Jordan added. Everyone started nodding, and we got the nod from Sean to make it happen. Just like that, it was on. Sunset paddle-out tonight, open invite.

By evening, what started as a ten-man send-off had blown up. Maybe a hundred or more people showed. Jordan and I passed out the extra leis we'd purchased to those who hadn't brought one. We paddled out on our boards, leis clenched in our teeth, making our way to a spot where Jordan waited. We sat cross-legged on our boards and joined hands to form a massive circle. In that circular formation, we placed the flowers on the water inside the circle formed by the noses of our boards, chanting, splashing, and churning the water. We stuck candles on the nose of our boards and lit them just as the sun descended and twilight gathered. A few words were spoken in honor of Colin, prayers were offered, and blessings were implored. In less than an hour, it was over. It had been a moving ceremony, and as darkness fell upon us, we turned around and headed back to shore, many of us feeling closure for the first time.

Feeling surprisingly good afterward, I picked up a couple of magazines spread around the lobby on my way back to my room. They were stacked at each end of the reception and concierge desks for guests to grab. I recognized our P.R. firm's fingerprints all over the ploy since Josh's picture was on the cover of most of them—either bold, front and center, or small and placed along the side. I took a couple with me, and once inside my room, I plopped down in the deep, comfortable chair by the windows, cracked open a bottle of water from the mini-fridge, and began perusing the articles.

A full portrait of Josh graced the cover of the June issue of Surf Rider, from weeks after he won the Ultimate Surfer title in Biarritz. The article's content was familiar—most journalists wrote the same thing—but I checked out the photos. There were at least a dozen high-def shots of all of us mugging for the camera. Me, Jordan, and Colin looking totally extreme—Colin with his bright ginger locks catching fire in the sun, me with my dark hair pulled into a wolf's tail, and Jordan's dreads in shades from bright gold to dark mahogany, looking very Bob Marley-like. The only thing we had in common were our huge smiles, all teeth and gums because we were cheesing so hard.

There was an action shot of Sean running out of the ocean, surfboard in hand after his heats, his long black hair catching the breeze, whipping behind him, and another of Colin jumping around on the sand, obviously stoked about whatever had just gone down. Colin was short compared to Sean, built like a wrestler, while Sean was tall, slim, and supremely agile. Colin had been a gentle bear. Not a Teddy bear, but more like Father Bear.

At the end of the article, there was a shot zooming in on Sean, Colin, and Josh in a huddle and another of the entire team seated in the sand in front of our boards, which were standing upright. They were probably some of the last shots taken of Colin and certainly the last of all of us together. We'd been super stoked after those big wins in Biarritz. Immediately after, Josh, Sean, and Colin took off for their long-awaited vacation—and the horror that awaited them.

The next couple of sports magazines carried the story of the shark attack. I flipped through those pictures quickly, not wanting to focus on the grizzly images. I'd been traumatized enough watching the story unfold in real-time. The last magazine carried the story of Josh's rehab, including a photo of a cute woman doctor in scrubs and a lab coat, standing by his side. She was the one who supposedly saved his life. *Dr. Mia Thomas,* the caption stated. It was a nice, proof-of-life picture of him as he tried to walk, holding on to parallel bars. She was beaming like he'd stolen home base. I closed the magazine and tossed it, along with the rest, onto the desk. Housekeeping would collect them in the morning.

CHAPTER THREE

Opening day was electric.

Sean was tipped to take it all in the Men's Masters Division, and just having him with us had the whole team jacked up. We were all buzzing, especially the squads gunning for the big kahuna and the Champion's Cup. The lineup was stacked—forty-four crews deep. Some teams rolled three deep, but our gang had a solid four: Sean was back on the roster, and Vince had stepped up to the number two spot, filling Colin's slot. Then Marc, followed by Joey Maldonado. Joey had hustled hard to snag that last open slot, beating out me, Jordan, Grayson, and Lloyd. At nineteen, Joey was the youngest on the team, but he wasn't called Cowboy for nothing. He was a real hustler, a show-off, and he had the skill to back it up. While we all had talent, Joey was fearless. Thrill rides were his bread and butter, and we needed his fearless edge to wow the judges if we were going to take the division honors.

Like most big competitions, the days were a mix of hurry-up-and-wait. Team and individual events were full-throttle, heart-pounding action interspersed with lots of waiting. Four-teen divisions were competing, with over two hundred athletes at the top of their game. There were two and four-person team events for the Junior Men and Women, the Intermediate Men and Women, and the Advanced Men and Women on the first two days. The Individual Men's and Women's events, at the same three levels, took place on the second and third days. The last day and a half was reserved for the Championship Men's and Women's events. Many competitors participated in multiple events at varying levels.

I had competed in the two-person team and the Men's Individual Intermediate event. I survived the elimination heats and would be back on the waves that afternoon. But in the meantime, I hung out at the shoreline, knee-deep in froth, cheering on my crew, still competing. When the spray settled, our boys crushed it, carving their names into the next lineup.

Josh was there too, but not to shred. He was working the charm offensive for the sponsors and building up the hype, doing his bit on the sidelines. I caught a glimpse of his mug grinning from the Jumbotron, chilling with the commentary crew—Kevin Collier, Lonnie Davis, and George Durant—because the crowd was going nuts. They loved him and showed it, their cheers like a wave of sound crashing over us. Josh lapped it up, stood tall, and gave a double-armed salute.

"Peep Josh hogging the limelight." Jeff jabbed me, thumbing back at the big screen.

"Playing the hype man? Not my scene," I said, shaking my

head. I couldn't imagine giving an impromptu interview to thousands of people live and on TV.

Jeff chuckled. "It ain't too shabby when you're tight with those boys."

Collier, the dude who used to rule the waves before trading his surfboard for a mic, was dissecting plays like the pro he once was. Davis's career had been cut short a few years back by a wack wipeout, which had been messed up. I remember going head-to-head with his team more than a few times before they broke up. Then there was Durant. He'd never shredded a wave competitively, but he climbed the media ladder to become the face of his own sports show.

Josh was killing it with them, looking like he was made for the camera—no shocker—and still riding the high from snagging his eighth World Title in Biarritz a few months back. He had plenty to talk about.

On day two, we were up with the dawn, buzzing despite barely clocking any shut-eye. Sixty bright-eyed souls lined up for our solo showdown, and I was itching to claim that big five-figure purse in the Men's Individuals. As we gathered, everyone's eyes were on the sky—gray and moody, thick thunderheads shrouding the sun. For a while, it seemed like the competition might be paused, but after a long deliberation among the officials, the competitors were given the all-clear. The waves were beasts determined not to be conquered by mere mortals. The crowd had more than doubled, spilling from the cliffs down to the crush at the surf line. Security was hustling, keeping the onlookers at bay. My number was thirty-eight—a long wait in the wings—so I snagged a front-row seat to watch them pull aerials and slice up the waves with slick moves. These were my competitors.

My turn was coming up soon when I heard a commotion further up the beach. I spotted Jeff in the thick of it, his blond mop sticking above the crowd. Some of our crew darted over, ready to dive into the melee, but I stayed put. My eyes were on the prize—I wasn't about to get sidetracked over a scuffle, even if Jeff was stirring it up—again.

Within minutes, it got bigger and more disorderly, and I was hard-pressed to stay focused. Surf. Scuffle. Surf...Then I heard my number called. That was my cue. I shoved the beach drama to the back of my mind because it was show time. I grabbed my board and hit the water, paddling out to the lineup. Three ahead, two bobbing behind, all of us champing at the bit for our shot. When it was my turn, I met the wave head-on. It was a beast, but I was ready. I hunkered down, found my line, and dropped in just as the wave curled over, tucking me into its barrel. I was in the pocket, riding the surge, battling to keep my edge.

Busting out of the barrel to the sight of sunlight winking off the water, I knew I nailed it—a stunner right off the bat. The buzz from that ride was unreal. I made my way to the beach, planted my board in the sand, and the props started rolling in— high fives and hoots from all over. My team, though? MIA. It was weird, but my head was all about the next wave.

Despite kicking off with a bang, the rest of my runs fizzled. By the end, I was out of the running, with no cash to show for it.

I headed back, feeling the sting of defeat. Walking into the hotel lobby, Vince caught me right away.

"Dude, where've you been?"

"Been at the beach, bro. Where else? What's the deal here?"

"Chaos, man. Beach brawl. We got snagged by security."

"It was Jeff, wasn't it?" I snapped.

"He and his trap can't ever just lay low."

"Surprisingly, nope. Some journo got in Josh's grill, things got nasty, and Jeff, well, he went full knockout on the guy and his camera buddy. Place turned into a free-for-all, and next thing, we were all stuck at the pavilion. The big wigs were this close to axing us from the comp."

"Seriously? How'd you wiggle out of that mess?"

"Josh, man. He's slick. Must've cut some kind of deal. We're still on. But Jeff's on lockdown, banned from the beach till the comp's done."

"That's nuts," I said, shocked and disgusted.

"Totally. You weren't there. I figured you'd dodged the bullet."

"Missed it by a hair. I was in the solo run when it kicked off. Caught a glimpse, then it was my turn to ride."

"Rough out there?"

"Didn't make the cut for the prize." I shrugged it off like it was nothing, but it still stung.

"Shame, man. Some of the guys are gonna cut loose tonight and shake off the drama. You in?"

"Pass. Gonna rinse off the day and chill. How about you?"

"Still tossing it up. Might hit the town, might not."

"I'm gonna pass. Catch you later."

"Sure thing. Later."

Riding the elevator up, I couldn't shake the image of the beach turning into a throwdown ring. Josh and a reporter? That was the last scene I'd expect. Reporters usually ate up whatever Josh dished out—not just because he's a champ many times over, but the guy's also rolling in it, splashed across every glossy mag worth a glance, and bankrolled by the kind of sponsors that make other surfers go green. What could've lit that fuse?

I had to get the lowdown, and Jordan was my go-to for the scoop—he had an ear in every conversation and eyes on every move. Once I got cleaned up, I was going to try to get all my questions answered.

~

The four days of events went as smoothly as butter, and the divisions were over. The final day dawned gloriously sunny, bright, and warm, and we gathered on the beach for the last competition—the Championship Cup. The initial forty-odd contenders had been whittled down to ten, with Sean top-seeded. Josh was MIA, but the rest of us were there to cheer Sean on for the win.

That evening, the hotel ballroom was transformed for a sumptuous dinner and dancing. Exotic perfumed flowers and fruit arrangements served as centerpieces and decorations.

Over a hundred and fifty round-top tables, covered in snow-white linens, crystal, and gold-rimmed china, filled the room. The walls of windows were open to the night, and a massive, double-sided fireplace on one side of the room threw enough warmth to counterbalance the ocean breeze. All the conference attendees had tickets to the dinner—a chance to greet old friends and make new ones.

I'd come down a little early to explore the hotel and maybe check out the gift shops, but I ran into Lloyd and Jordan chatting with a group of girls. They flagged me over and introduced me to the ladies, who were members of the Women's Surf Division. We chitchatted for a few minutes, standing in the middle of the breezeway, before deciding it might be better to move out of the way of foot traffic. I asked the ladies if they'd like to find a table for dinner, and we all sat together near the open expanse overlooking the lanai and the ocean beyond. Somehow, I ended up between two young ladies who seemed to be good friends.

Sarena was Brazilian, from Rio, with a thick accent that made her chatter both charming and a little hard to decipher. The other one, Carey, was from South Africa, near the Cape. Both were on the same team and champion surfers, and this was their first trip to the United States. I asked if they were spending any extra time here after the competition, maybe doing a little sightseeing, but they were leaving early the next morning. They still had a couple more competitions before finishing up the year in Jeffrey's Bay, South Africa. We'd be heading out to J-Bay next month, too, finishing our year-long tour at Bells Beach in Victoria, Australia. We kept the conversation light, mostly focusing on the competitions we'd all been in, how everyone was doing on the waves, and how their year-to-date scores were shaking out.

After dinner, the waitstaff cleared away all traces of the banquet, and a live band took over. Our group meandered out onto the lanai and the beach, where soft Hawaiian music played. A huge bonfire crackled down by the surf, throwing shadows that danced on the sand like sea spirits. Laughter bubbled up, coming from everywhere on the beach, as spontaneous and capricious as the ocean breeze. A couple of guys wrestled in the sand, their buddies betting on the outcome, while others tossed foam footballs back and forth, their whoops and hollers punctuating the night air. I heard a guitar being strummed and a man singing in accompaniment, with people clapping to the beat. We headed that way, and before I knew it, my foot tapped along with the music, my body finding the rhythm.

Like kids, some people were running around passing out sticks stabbed through the center of marshmallows. Grayson, as excited as a big kid himself, snagged a few and handed each of us one, his grin as wide as the board he rode.

"I haven't roasted a marshmallow since I was a kid," he said, his voice rough with salt and wind.

We took our treats over toward the bonfire and sat in front of one of the smaller fire pits on many of the blankets scattered about. I held my stick above the embers, rotating the marshmallow, watching it bloat and brown, then tried to eat the sticky, gooey mess without dropping it or burning my mouth. It was a simple pleasure but as satisfying as a well-ridden wave.

Someone started a game of volleyball a few feet away, and the ball came soaring over the net, landing with a soft thud near my feet. I picked it up, feeling the gritty sand against my fingers, and we jumped into the game. My movements were spontaneous and exhilarating—a dive, a high-five, the sting of the ball against my palm—all under the gaze of a thousand stars.

There was a shout, "Quinn, to you!" and I launched the ball back over the net, my competitive edge sharpened by the day's defeat and soothed by the night's camaraderie. This was different; there was no prize, no judges, just the pure joy of the game.

After a few rounds, I was hot and thirsty, so I retreated from the game, my breaths deep with the tang of salt air. I got a fresh beer, the liquid cool against my throat, and let out a contented sigh. Laughter, the hiss of surf, the crackle of fire— it was all here, the symphony of a surfer's celebration. The volleyball rolled toward me again, and I tossed it back into the game with a wave, indicating I was out. Boos and hisses greeted my decision, but the game continued without me.

The next morning, most of us slept in, hungover from a night of heavy celebrating. Although I hadn't had more than a couple of beers, I didn't crawl out of bed until it was almost time to check out. Luckily, I'd thrown my things together last night before going out with the guys and only needed to shower, get dressed, and check out before meeting up with the crew downstairs. Sean had called a team meeting for one o'clock in the Dolphin Room, and I had plenty of time to run to the little burger joint around the corner for an old-fashioned, half-pound American cheeseburger with mustard, ketchup, pickles, lettuce, tomatoes, and grilled onions—and a sack of crispy fries. I'd eaten there every day of the tournament, and after more than a year out of the country, I couldn't get enough. They just didn't make burgers—and they just didn't taste the same—anywhere else in the world like they did in the States. Just the thought made my mouth water and my stomach grumble.

CHAPTER
FOUR

After lunch, once everyone had checked out of the hotel, we met in the Dolphin Room before loading onto the bus that would take us back to Los Angeles International Airport.

I dropped my gear next to the mountain of expensive equipment and designer luggage the others had piled up against the wall and pulled up a chair at the bare, marble-topped conference table between Jordan and Joey.

"Okay," Sean started, his tone lacking its usual warm camaraderie. Today, he was all business, crisp and firm. "I think we're all here. We won't take up much of your time, but Josh and I wanted to talk to you before we head out."

Josh stood up, his face a mask of professionalism that didn't quite reach his eyes. "I wish we were meeting under different circumstances," he said, his voice steady but somber. He looked over at Sean, who continued with a heavy sigh, "The long and short of it, guys... is that we're disbanding the team. This last year hit our finances harder than we expected. We're out of reserves, and almost all of our big sponsors have declined to renew our contracts."

A collective gasp sucked the air out of the room. Disbanding? The word ricocheted around inside my skull. This team was my family, my identity.

I felt my grip tighten on the armrests, my knuckles whitening. We'd ridden waves together, celebrated victories, and supported each other through wipe-outs. And now, just like that, we were washed ashore.

Sean made eye contact with each of us before continuing. "We've managed to pull together severance for you all. Josh has been very generous, and I think you'll find it's more than fair." He fanned a stack of envelopes in his hand, then passed them to Josh.

The silence that followed was suffocating. Josh took the envelopes and moved around the table, handing each of us one. His movements were mechanical. When he reached me, our eyes met briefly—a flicker of mutual pain—and he handed me the envelope with my name handwritten across the middle, then moved on.

Sean kept speaking. "We'll do all we can to help you get on other teams or make other arrangements. You have our numbers. Feel free to use them."

Holding the envelope in my hand felt like a betrayal. Inside was a check, a generous amount, as Sean had said, but it felt like a consolation prize for a game I never agreed to play.

Done dispensing the envelopes, Josh returned to his place at the table, standing in front of his chair. He cleared his throat. "We've loved every minute with you guys. This is the hardest decision I've ever had to make."

The room was full of murmurs now, a low tide of disbelief and despair. I couldn't speak, couldn't look up. The walls of the conference room felt like they were closing in. The future I had envisioned was being unceremoniously ripped away, leaving behind a void as vast and unforgiving as the ocean during a storm.

I stared down at the envelope in my hand, its weight of it like a stone. The paper crackled—a sound that seemed too loud in the thick silence that followed the bombshell. Disbanded! The word bounced around in my head, a cruel echo.

My heart pounded a fierce rhythm, like when dropping into a towering wave, but now it was fear, not adrenaline, surging through my veins. The air felt heavy, charged with a collective shock that buzzed in my ears and blurred the faces around me.

I squeezed the envelope, the sharp edges pressing into my palm, grounding me in the harsh reality. This thin packet of paper was the full stop at the end of a long, shared sentence. I couldn't open it; to do so would be to acknowledge the finality of it all.

I looked up as Josh and Sean stood there, the weight of their decision carved into the lines of their faces. They were our leaders, the ones who had always navigated us through rough waters, and now they were beaching the ship for good.

I tried to swallow, but my throat was tight, constricted by a swell of emotions. Around me, I heard the rustle of others opening their envelopes, the soft sniffs of those struggling to keep their composure. But I was frozen, the envelope clutched in a vice grip, a lifeline that felt more like an anchor dragging me down.

My eyes met Josh's again, and he leaned forward.

"If you ever need anything, Quinn, call me. We're still family. We'll always be family."

I forced myself to hold his gaze, forcing back the tears. He had to know how much disbanding the team gutted us. I don't know about the others, but I would've stuck with them no matter what. But no words could fix this. No apologies could stitch together the ripped seams of our family. He patted my shoulder and moved on, and I sat motionless, staring at nothing. Silence settled on the room, heavy as the ocean's depths, and in the darkness and silence, I gripped the arms of my chair, my mind racing as frenetic as a storm across the sea. My teammates were shifting, some standing, others clutching their own envelopes like life preservers, but my envelope lay in my lap, unopened. I couldn't go home—not like this, not with a cargo of broken dreams and few options.

My family, my old life—they were a world away. A small coastal community where everyone knew your name and your business. A place I'd left behind with dreams of making it big, of riding waves to glory and bringing back fortunes. The thought of returning, not as the prodigal son made good, but as a castaway, was a bitter pill to swallow. It stuck in my throat.

I couldn't go back to stay with my family, no better than my brother. And I couldn't look into my father's hard, accusing eyes and admit that I had nothing to show for the five years I've been away. It wasn't just pride; it was fear—fear of disappointment, of pity, of being that cautionary tale told to wide-eyed children with their own dreams of leaving.

The room slowly began to empty, a slow exodus of somber figures, bags and boards slung over shoulders, quiet goodbyes muttered. I barely noticed them leaving. The coach bus that brought us here was waiting in front of the hotel to take us back to LAX if that was where we needed to go. Some were scrambling to arrange flights, purchase tickets home, or somewhere close to home. We were no longer on the league's roster—no hotel rooms were reserved for us, and there were no prearranged, prepaid flights to take us anywhere. We were on our own. The only silver lining was that I was back in the States, in California, but I didn't have a home to go back to. My gaze fixed on the grain of the wooden table, seeing in its pattern the swirls, eddies, and currents of the ocean, feeling as adrift as a skiff lost at sea.

I stood up abruptly, my chair scraping against the floor, the back slamming down with a loud, painful crack. With a deep breath, I stuffed the envelope into my backpack without looking at it. I'd deal with it later when I was alone, and the reality wouldn't sting quite as much. For now, I needed to move, to walk, to breathe. I left the room without looking back.

CHAPTER
FIVE

Angrily, I stomped past the reception area on my way out, the sliding doors whispering open for me before whooshing softly behind.

Instead of getting on the bus for LAX with the others, I trudged down the sidewalk, feeling crushed. The smack of my heels against the pavement was a metronome to my sinking spirits. I flagged down a taxi and asked the driver to take me to a motel off the strip but still close to the ocean.

"Where do you want to go?" he asked.

"The farther, the better," I replied. "And the cheaper, the better."

I settled in the back seat, slouching deep into the worn upholstery. My hand brushed against an old, frayed card stuck in the seat cushion. I pulled it out—it was some sort of advertisement, and at the bottom was a plug for the Cloverleaf Motel. Under new management, it said. I handed it to the driver, who looked at me quizzically.

"Is it by the ocean?"

"Looks like it from the address. Ocean Drive."

"Can you drop me there?"

"Sure. It's going to cost you."

"How much?"

"Seventy bucks if I turn off the meter."

"Yeah, okay. Do it."

I slouched back, staring out the window as the familiar sights of the city slipped away, replaced by the drab, faded outskirts. When we finally stopped, we were in front of a motel that looked like it had given up on life a decade ago. The sign, with half its lights flickering out of existence, seemed to nod at me in solidarity. The driver looked at me, and for a moment, I almost wanted to get back in the taxi. Instead, I nodded and paid him, tipping generously. We unloaded all of my gear, and he helped me hoist it onto my back and shoulders, except for the heavy duffel, which I carried with the straps wrapped in my fist.

I pushed open the door to the cramped office, where the smell of cigarette smoke and pine cleaner waged a silent war. The gleam of marble floors and decorated walls I'd come to expect in hotels was nowhere in sight, replaced by marred, ugly green walls and dull, cracked linoleum tiles. I winced. At the reception desk, a bored clerk glanced up, his eyes as flat as the rickety, caged counter that separated us.

"Need a room?" he asked, as if the answer could be anything but yes in a place people only came to forget.

I nodded, peeling a couple of bills from the wad of cash in my pocket. I thought it wise to keep my bank and credit cards in my wallet. The clerk nodded as I counted the bills with a snap of each note, the sound hitting me in my gut, punctuating my fall from grace. This place was a world away from the one I'd become too comfortable in.

"Room eight," he said, sliding a worn key across the counter with my receipt. "You've got a week."

I nodded and looked at the paper in my hand. 634 Ocean Drive. San Nobel, California. I laughed softly. A pretentious address for a ramshackle place like this. Struggling somewhat to back out of the hovel of an office, I was relieved to find Room Eight halfway down the narrow hall, just steps from the office. The door stuck slightly, probably warped in the frame, and it squealed as I pushed it open. Inside was a capsule of neglect—stains on the carpet telling tales of previous occupants, a bed that had seen better days, and a tiny lamp that was more a beacon of despair than of light.

I set my bags and boards down on the bed rather than the floor and sat on the edge beside them, the springs creaking in protest. I took in the details of the ten-by-ten cell, each one a hammer blow to my life. There wasn't much to see. The walls were the same ugly green; the carpet had once been light brown, an imitation of the sand outside the window. Warped metal blinds hung at the single window. Instead of a light citrusy perfume filling the air, the room smelled stale and musty.

With a sigh, I stood up and walked to the window, pulling the string to lift the blinds so I could open the window and let in some fresh air. Outside, the beach shimmered in the afternoon sun. A vast expanse of sand and water, a stark, abandoned landscape with waves rolling in like a tempest. Yet, they were no match for the bleakness of this room.

I ground down on my back teeth to keep from uttering a scream that was climbing up my throat. I'd just walked out of the embrace of a lavish, gilded world and stepped into a purgatory of my own making. With a resolute breath, I dropped the blinds and turned away from the window and the siren call of the ocean.

Tonight, I'd stay in Room Eight, but tomorrow? Maybe tomorrow would look better, and I might feel up to finding someplace else to stay. I couldn't imagine what it was like before new management took over. The motel was quiet, almost too quiet, and the silence weighed on me, but I couldn't bring myself to leave just yet.

Over the next few days, Jordan called me non-stop, leaving voicemails that ranged from concerned to borderline frantic. I could practically hear the worry in his voice as he tried to piece together where I was and why I'd disappeared without saying anything.

"Quinn, man, you gotta call me back. Where the hell are you? Nobody's heard from you. Just… just let me know you're okay, alright?"

Another call: "Quinn, come on, bro. Whatever it is, we can figure it out together. You don't have to do this alone."

I couldn't bring myself to answer. What would I even say? That I couldn't handle it? That the weight of everything was crushing me? Jordan was dealing with his own mess, barely holding it together, and the last thing he needed was to carry my burdens too. Every time I saw his name flash on the screen, I felt the pull of guilt gnawing at me. He was like a brother to me, and I hated knowing I was putting him through this.

The calls kept coming. Finally, I picked up, clearing my throat and trying to sound steady.

"Hey, Jo. Sorry, I've been, uh, busy. Didn't mean to worry you."

"Busy? Quinn, you just up and vanished. I've been calling everybody, trying to find you. Where are you, man?"

"I'm… I'm with family," I lied, hoping the words sounded convincing. "Just needed to get away for a bit, you know? Clear my head."

There was a pause on the other end, and I could tell he wasn't buying it. But he didn't push. That was Jordan—he knew when to press and when to let it go.

"Yeah, okay. Just, uh, don't ghost me, alright? We're all we got, man. You need anything, you call me."

"Thanks, Jo. I will."

We hung up, and I sat there, staring at my phone. I hated lying to him, but I couldn't let him see me like this—lost, drifting, without a clue of what to do next. The truth was, I was scared he'd see right through me and know I was barely hanging on. I knew I couldn't stay hidden away forever, but for now, the Cloverleaf Motel felt like the only place I could breathe.

My days became indistinguishable except for the changing guard of the sun and moon. A week became two, then three, and I was still living in Room Eight after a month. I had come to know every contour of the shoreline outside my window by heart—the way it curled into the ocean's embrace like a lover resigned to a tumultuous affair.

Dressed in a wetsuit as the water cooled with the fading summer, my board always in hand, I surfed day and night, escaping my thoughts and my room. The motel key dangled against my chest from a frayed lanyard around my neck. It was a lifeline, though I preferred the openness of the sky to the four walls that seemed to close in on me, reminding me of my broken circumstances. I'd return when I was too tired to do anything but sleep or when the pain and anger crept too close, and only the solidity of a locked door could hold them at bay.

Sometimes, I looked for work—odd jobs with flexible hours that would allow me to surf when I wanted. I avoided the surf shops in case someone might recognize me. I wasn't famous, but in some circles, I was known as the protégé, groomed to take over the circuit when the big Kahunas retired. No one needed to know I'd washed out. So, I spent my days as a silent silhouette drifting along the shoreline, my footsteps erased by the tide as if I were a ghost haunting the space between land and sea. San Nobel felt like a place in between. A fall from the heavens, but not yet swallowed by the sea. Hovering somewhere in the in-between.

At night, I'd sit outside on a tuft of seagrass or a secluded dune, my jacket pulled tight against the sea breeze. I'd stare up at the cosmos, wondering if the stars held any destiny for me or if they were just distant eyes watching me spiral out. Shadow people flickered at the periphery of my vision—a family or two, small children laughing and playing in the sand and surf; joggers chasing the next endorphin high; owners bringing their dogs out for exercise; lovers entwined in the sweet naivety of bliss. I stayed apart from them, a solitary figure cast adrift in the wake of a personal storm. Late in the evenings, small groups of homeless men and women came and went, some staying a night or two on the beach before city police rousted them off. With their weathered faces and knowing eyes, they would see me and nod but never encroach. They recognized a man on the edge of himself. I was one of them in spirit, yet not ready to accept their solidarity as one of the lost.

My reflections were my only conversation. I raged at the ocean, at the indifferent sky, at the relentless sand that couldn't give me a firm footing. I'd throw stones into the waves, each one a question, a curse, a plea. But the ocean swallowed my anger and soothed my relentlessness. With each passing day, I began to find refuge in the tides that were once as familiar as the rhythm of my heartbeat.

Every morning, I took my board out and lost myself to the waves under a sky painted in hues of indifference. The rest of the day, I was held in the grip of depression and desolation. My cash was almost gone, spent on the crappy room and dinners from the restaurants lining the boardwalk. If I couldn't find a job to keep me afloat, I'd have to dip into my stash. My anger over the nosedive my life had taken was beginning to wane, leaving only the gritty taste of reality. I was choking on it.

Sitting outside, in front of the motel, in a metal fold-up lawn chair, I watched as the waves clawed at the shore. The local surfers were absent, and the beach was abandoned except for me and the scavenging birds. I pulled my knees close, the fabric of my shorts damp from the sand and ocean spray, and let my gaze roam over the unending cycle of the waves, a constant push and pull that mirrored the war within me. Today, they sounded like a chorus of disapproval in my father's voice, a constant reminder that I was destined for nothing. The severance check, hidden away in my duffel bag at the back of that dingy motel closet, served as undeniable proof that he might have been right all along. Damn, I thought. I'd wanted him to be wrong. Leaving home had been my attempt to defy him and his expectations, but out here, by myself, even the wind held no comfort, and the soothing melody of the sea couldn't drown out my doubts.

I realized I was still, unconsciously, fighting against the tides. I hadn't let go. I hadn't given in to the weight of my despair, even though the temptation to do so whispered to me with each wave, as seductive as a siren's call. So many times, I could have taken my surfboard and drifted out beyond the breakers, letting the waves take me wherever they would. There was a strange comfort in the thought of surrender, in the thought of being swallowed by the vastness of the ocean. Yet, deep inside the depths of my being, like a cable buried on the ocean floor, was a thread of something raw, unfrayed, and unbroken. Pain, rejection, and defeat were hollowing me out, yet it was there—a lifeline waiting for me to grab hold of and pull myself up. Touching it cautiously, I felt a jolt, the electric sizzle of possibility.

I didn't have to end up a footnote in my own story, a cautionary tale whispered among the waves. Hope bubbled up and shimmered around me, as ethereal yet as real and as bright as the light of the stars. I could make it on my own. It wouldn't be easy, of course. Nothing ever was. But I'd made it this far in my life. I could make it the rest of the way. A setback didn't mean defeat. The ocean in front of me, with its relentless crashes and retreats, was proof that even after the harshest storm, the tide still turned.

With a resolve that surprised even me, I stood, and the waves acknowledged my decision with thunderous applause. Tomorrow was uncertain, the future unwritten, but I decided I would meet it head-on, with the tenacity of the sea and the courage of a man who had nothing left to lose—and everything to prove. With a final look at the waves, their hypnotic dance under the waxing moonlight indifferent but constant, I picked up my folding chair and carried it back inside my room.

I woke the next morning to the distant wail of a siren. The room was dimly lit, the blinds doing their best to keep out the unforgiving morning sun. My motel room had seen better days, like a man down on his luck. The cracked paint on the walls whispered stories of countless travelers who had passed through, leaving behind their own trail of troubles. With a heavy sigh, I swung my legs over the edge of the creaky bed. It was time to get my act together—or at least try. I couldn't let my life dwindle away day by day without a fight.

Dragging myself to the bathroom, I caught my reflection in the ancient, faded mirror on the medicine cabinet door. Tired eyes stared back at me. I needed a steaming hot shower to wash off the stink of desperation and despair or at least make me believe I was starting with a clean slate. But the water here was tepid at best, and I'd have to make do. I stepped into the shower, letting the lukewarm water pour over me, and my mind wandered. Today, I'd give the job hunt a fair chance. While I was out, I'd look for a budget-friendly place to stay, something that wouldn't drain my bank account and wouldn't make me feel like I was dwelling in the shade of failure. It didn't need to be lavish—just a solid roof over my head and within walking distance of the ocean. I also needed to snatch back my pride. I was a damn good surfer, and getting shucked off by Josh and Sean wasn't something I could control.

I reached for the half-empty bottle of shampoo, squeezing out every last drop as if it held the answers to all my problems. The suds ran down my body, carrying away the shame and the pain. The light bulb in my head flashed. I shouldn't have been ashamed to be let go. Being kicked to the curb wasn't my fault— the team's financial problems weren't something I could control. If I needed to take the blame for something, it was getting in too deep and never figuring it could happen to me. Yep, I'd gone into it with eyes wide shut. Wasn't that a movie? It didn't matter. What mattered was never again. From this point on, I was on my own, and that meant I needed to be in control of my destiny. I began to scrub with vigor, turning my skin red. A new day. A lesson learned.

After the shower, I felt a little more buoyant, determined to get on with my day. I finished drying off and dressed in some slightly less wrinkled cargo shorts and a vintage long-sleeved T-shirt that had to be thirty years old. I took a last look around the dingy motel room, seeing all my stuff scattered around, trying to trick me into thinking this was home, and wondered if I was forgetting anything. Assuming not, I locked the door and stepped out into a brighter world.

The glass bank doors slid open, and a blast of frigid air hit me the moment I stepped inside. The place was bustling with activity, a stark contrast to my life over the past month and a half. I approached the line, clutching my severance check with attitude. Fortunately, this was a branch of the bank where I had an account, and all I needed to do was deposit it. I could have done it at the rack of ATMs outside the door, but there were only a few people in line, and I had nothing but time on my hands.

Finally, it was my turn. I stepped up to the counter and offered a flirtatious smile to the young woman behind the glass. She was cute, and she gave me a polite smile back.

"Hi, I'd like to deposit this check," I said, stepping up to the window.

"Yes, sir, I can help you with that. Do you have an account with us? If so, may I see your debit card and ID?"

I tossed my bank card and California driver's license onto the ledge and opened the envelope while she typed furiously on her keyboard. The check was written for fifty-five thousand dollars. I swallowed hard and cleared my throat, catching her looking at my license and then back at me as if she was trying to tell if the crappy picture on the license was really me.

"Uhm, I must have forgotten the check," I muttered, suddenly reluctant to part with it. "I thought I had it with me. Can you just give me a balance?"

"On which accounts, Mr. Lawler?"

"Uhm, all of them, I guess."

She started typing again, and I carefully folded the envelope with the check inside so that it didn't slip out and stuffed it into my wallet. I couldn't part with the check. It wasn't just the money—if I cashed it, it would feel like I'd been severed from everything I've come to know.

"Here you go, Mr. Lawler," she said, pushing three receipts and my cards across the ledge to me. "Your checking, savings, and investment accounts. Is there anything else I can assist you with today?"

I shook my head, giving her another playful smile. "No, thank you, Joanna," I said, reading her badge. "That's all for now." She smiled back at me, a little more genuinely this time.

Walking out of the bank, I looked at my balances. I knew what they were; I checked them regularly on the app on my phone. Altogether, I had close to seven hundred fifty thousand dollars. I could hold on to Josh's check a little longer.

Feeling optimistic that I'd be able to find a decent place to rent before my week was up at the motel, I headed toward the beach, intending to walk down to the huddle of shops at the far end. My belly started growling about halfway down, reminding me I hadn't eaten since yesterday morning, and Harry's Seafood

Shack seemed like a good place to grab a sandwich. A faded sign in the window caught my eye, and I pushed the door open. The interior was cozy, with nautical-themed decorations adorning ship-lapped walls. I approached the counter, where a tall, athletically-built Black man with alert eyes and a wry smile watched me.

"Yessir, can I get something for you?" His voice was soft for such a big man, and he had a distinctively southern inflection.

"Hey there," I said, trying to sound friendly. "I saw the 'Help Wanted' sign in the window. Mind if I inquire about the position?"

The man looked me up and down, his thick lips twitching as if considering his words carefully. "Well, I'm looking' for someone who ain't afraid to get their hands dirty and knows a thing or two about seafood. You got any restaurant experience?"

I nodded. "Yeah, a little. I bussed and washed dishes part-time while I was in high school. I can also handle myself around the kitchen."

The man raised an eyebrow. "Good to hear. Name's Harry, by the way. I run this place. What's your name?"

"Quinn. Quinn Lawler."

"You're kinda new around here, aren't you, Quinn Lawler? Tell me, why are you looking for a job here? You planning on staying a while?"

I hesitated for a moment, deciding how much I wanted to tell him. "Yeah, I'm the fresh face 'round here. Life kinda tossed me a wild one recently, so I'm just looking to plant my feet under me again. Figured this spot is as chill as any to make that happen."

Harry scratched his bristled chin and gave me a thoughtful look. "It's just me around here, ten hours a day, seven days a week. I close up for a couple of hours after the lunch rush, take a breather, you know? Now that the summer season is over, it'll probably be kinda quiet out here, but I've got a lot of little projects that need doing. You okay with doing some fixer-up projects?"

"Yeah. Probably better at that than cooking, to tell the truth."

"You do some of the projects, and I can get away without hiring another cook. What d'ya think?"

"Sounds killer, Harry."

"Tell you what, Quinn Lawler, how 'bout you come back tomorrow morning…ten o'clock, for a trial shift? We'll see if you're a good fit for the Shack."

Relief washed over me as I extended my hand to shake his. "Major thanks for the chance, but you don't have to call me by my whole name, Harry. My mama's the only person to do that, and only when she's pissed with me. I'm okay with Quinn if that's okay with you."

He flashed a wide smile, revealing a double row of large, white teeth. "Okay, Quinn. But don't thank me yet. We'll see if you can handle the heat in the kitchen."

I smiled back as Harry returned to wiping things down. However, I was still hungry.

"Hey, Harry. Gimme two deluxe fish sandwiches and an order of fries."

"You want a fountain drink or a can of soda? You want it to go?"

"Fountain, please, and I think I'll just post up over there and scope out the scene."

The food was delicious, or I was hungry enough that even the wrapper would have tasted good. When I left Harry's, my spirits were lifted. Maybe this was what I needed—something to do, to focus on. Perhaps the future wouldn't feel so uncertain.

CHAPTER
SIX

The next morning, I arrived at Harry's, determined to make the most of my fresh start.

Harry looked like he'd been there all morning, and the "Help Wanted" sign was gone from the window. I greeted him with a big grin.

"Morning, Quinn," he said, acknowledging my eagerness.

"Ready to get to work?"

I nodded, the anticipation of a new beginning coursing through me. "Definitely," I replied as he led me around to the kitchen. My first task was to prepare the day's seafood catch. I donned an apron and gloves, then started shucking oysters, deveining shrimp, and scaling and filleting the fish. You can't grow up in a small town off the ocean without learning how to catch, clean, and cook seafood. And Harry mostly used fresh. It was a messy job, but I embraced it, finding a strange satisfaction in the rhythm of the work.

As the lunch hour approached, the restaurant began to fill with hungry customers. I was handed the reins of the fryer, tasked with ensuring the golden crispiness of the clam strips, shrimp, and fries. The sizzle of the hot oil, the gentle chatter of the patrons, and the clinking of cutlery became a calm backdrop to the work.

During the lunch rush, I worked alongside Harry, deftly assembling the carry-out orders and the little red baskets for the patrons eating inside. Then I went out, cleaned the tables, straightened the chairs, and emptied the garbage. The eat-in area wasn't that big, so it was a no-brainer what needed to be done. I didn't have to wait for Harry to tell me. After the lunchtime frenzy subsided, it was time to mop up. I scrubbed pots and pans, mopped the floors, and wiped down every surface, leaving the kitchen and restaurant sparkling. Harry was impressed with my diligence.

"You're not afraid to get your hands dirty, Quinn. That's a good sign."

As the afternoon wore on, I noticed a leaky faucet in the restroom. With a wrench in hand, I tackled the small repair job, feeling a sense of accomplishment as I tightened the pipes and stopped the dripping. It reminded me of fixing things around the house, where there'd always been something needing attention. At the end of my shift, Harry and I stepped outside the Shack and savored the sun and the warm, golden glow it cast over the beach. It had been a long and uneventful eight hours, and I was pleasantly tired, but I couldn't help wondering if I had done enough to secure the job. Harry leaned against the weathered siding of the frame building, a faint smile tugging at the corners of his lips.

"Quinn," he began, his gaze fixed on the fading light dancing on the water, "I've seen a lot of folks come through here over the years, but not many have the kind of grit you showed today."

I shifted on my feet, my heart pounding in my chest as I waited for his verdict. The ocean waves soothed the tension in the air.

He turned to me, his eyes locking onto mine. "So, I just wanted to let you know—you've got the job if you want it."

The weight of his words hung in the air for a moment before they fully registered. Relief and gratitude surged through me, and a smile spread across my face. "Thank you, Harry. I really appreciate this opportunity."

Harry laughed loudly, a hearty sound that seemed to come from the depths of his being. "No need to thank me, Quinn. You earned it. We'll start you off part-time, and see how things go. But I have a feeling you'll do just fine here."

I couldn't have been happier. It was more than a job; it was a lifeline, a chance to get on my feet. I extended my hand, and Harry shook it warmly. "Welcome to the Seafood Shack, Quinn," he said with a wink.

"But we need to talk about your hours," Harry added, his expression sincere but apologetic. "With the tourist season winding down, it ain't going to be too busy in the evenings pretty soon, especially when the shops down here close and it starts getting dark early."

I nodded, disappointment tugging at the edges of my enthusiasm. "Yeah, sure, I get it, Harry. I'm just grateful for the opportunity you've given me."

Harry's face softened, and he placed a hand on my shoulder. "I knew you'd understand. You work the morning shift and cut after the lunch rush. How's that? When things pick up again, you can get more hours."

I smiled, though I was a little concerned about making ends meet without dipping into my checking account. However, the hours sounded perfect, and I did like it here, which counted for a lot.

"Thanks, Harry. I'll make the most of the time you give me."

The Shack, as Harry referred to the restaurant, and now had me referring to it in the same way, was not too far from the motel—about a thirty-minute walk at a fast clip. I'd get up at dawn, take my board out for a couple of hours, shower, and head out to work. I was barely making minimum wage and getting paid weekly, but it was okay. The work was easy and more social than anything. I got to meet the regulars, most of whom lived and worked in the area, and a few of the surfers I'd seen on the water over the past month and a half. When Harry handed me my second check, I figured it was time to move out of the Cloverleaf for real. I still had my first paycheck and the severance check, and I put the paycheck Harry had just handed me inside the envelope with them.

I hadn't seen any apartments for rent close by, which meant I either had to walk farther to work or the ocean. That meant no doubling back to shower and dress after my morning surf before coming in to work unless I took taxis or rideshares. I didn't care for that, so the other option was to stay at the Cloverleaf or move into a nicer hotel or motel. Despite what one might think, that decision wasn't all that easy. Yeah, the Cloverleaf was a dump, but it was affordable, and it was close. Some of the other cheap motels would run almost eighteen hundred dollars a month, the price of a one-bedroom apartment with a kitchen and hot water.

"Hey, Harry," I said, walking over to the order counter and leaning on it with both elbows. "Do you happen to know of any cheap places to rent around here? I've been looking for a place to rent close by, but I haven't found anything within walking distance. I really gotta get outta the Cloverleaf Motel."

"The Cloverleaf down the way?"

"Yeah, that dump."

Harry scratched his beard, contemplating for a moment.

"Well, Quinn, kinda funny you should ask. I've got a little studio over the garage behind here that I've been using for storage. It's not much. Three rooms my ex-wife set up as a studio space where she painted. She was an artist."

"Really?" My eyes widened in surprise. I hadn't expected such an offer. "You'd be willing to rent it to me?"

Harry nodded, a genuine smile on his face. "Course, it needs some work and some furniture to make it cozy. It's been sitting empty for a while now. I can even throw in the rent as part of your pay. That could save me a little bit of cash."

I couldn't believe my luck. My own place, on the waterfront. It was a lifeline. I'd have my own space without making withdrawals from the bank every week. "Harry, I don't know what to say. Thanks a lot, Dude. A job and a place. Wow, it's perfect."

He waved his hand dismissively. "No need to thank me. It's just three little rooms, and it needs cleaning out and cleaning up before you can move in."

"I can start this afternoon getting it cleaned up, Harry, if that's alright with you. The Cloverleaf charges by the week, and maybe I won't need another week there."

"Yeah, sure. Let's go take a look."

Harry locked up the restaurant, put a sign on the door telling customers we'd be right back, and led me through a narrow path behind the Seafood Shack, across a small square courtyard to a small building at the back of the property. The studio apartment was perched over the garage, a quaint and weathered structure that looked sturdy but also like it had seen its fair share of seasons.

"Here we are, Quinn," Harry said, unlocking the door with an old brass key. He swung it open, revealing a steep set of stairs that led up to the apartment. "It ain't much, but it's got potential."

I stepped inside, taking in the space. It was divided into three rooms: a modest living area with a window that had a nice view of the ocean above the rooftops, a galley kitchen with a small dining nook, and a bathroom with a bedroom that had a door. The place had character, but it definitely needed some love.

"It's perfect," I said with a genuine smile, appreciating the opportunity more with each passing moment. "I can see myself making this place comfortable."

Harry smiled. "Glad you like it, Quinn. Now, I should warn you, it hasn't been lived in for a while, so it'll need some cleaning and maybe a fresh coat of paint."

I nodded, not at all deterred by the prospect of a little DIY. "I don't mind that at all, Harry. It shouldn't take but a few hours to clean it out, and I can take care of the painting after work once I'm in."

Harry seemed pleased with my willingness to put in the effort. "That sounds fair to me. You're handy in the kitchen, and it looks like you've got some skills with a broom and a paintbrush, too. Here's the key. It's yours now."

We continued to inspect the apartment, discussing the logistics of the move and what supplies I might need. The more we talked, the more grateful I felt for the chance Harry had given me. It was more than a place to live; it was a fresh start and a place to rebuild my life.

The rest of the afternoon, I couldn't help but feel a sense of excitement and hope. I was ready to roll up my sleeves, clean, paint, and make that little space my own. It was a sign that I was in the right place at the right time. I'd been given a chance to set a new course for my life, and I was determined to make the most of it.

Every day after work, I went straight to the apartment. Harry had given me some large trash bags and told me I could use anything I needed. There was some furniture stacked up in the garage below, and I dragged out all kinds of things into the courtyard to take stock. I intended to fix up a table, a couple of chairs, and a bright orange futon that I could use as a couch. It needed a new cover, but I could make do with a blanket or something.

Harry needed to make a quick run to the market, and I hopped in the car with him. I needed a few things for the apartment. He dropped me off, and when I was done, he'd be there to pick me up. When I stepped out of the small hardware store, pushing several bags for my apartment project in a cart, I saw Harry had parked the car in front of the store, but he wasn't back yet. I shrugged. I hadn't seen much of the town yet, so I could wait and people-watch. He probably wouldn't be much longer. As I stood on the sidewalk, a familiar face caught my eye. It was the girl, the bank teller from the other day—Joanna. I smiled, remembering her name, and her steps slowed as she recognized me.

She offered a friendly smile. "Hey. Quinn, right?"

I nodded, returning her smile. "That's me. And you're...?" I teased, acting like I didn't know.

She laughed, extending her hand. "I'm Joanna Singleton, the teller who helped you at the bank."

I shook her hand, appreciating the chance encounter. "Nice to officially meet you, Joanna Singleton. What brings you here?"

She motioned to the street. "Just running some errands. And you?"

I gestured to the bags of supplies. "I'm fixing up my new apartment. I got a little job at the Seafood Shack."

Joanna's eyes lit up with interest. "That sounds like a fun project. Is it your first time doing something like this?"

I nodded again, feeling a sense of camaraderie with this unexpected acquaintance. "Yeah, first time in a long time. But I'm looking forward to it."

We chatted for a few more minutes about DIY projects and the challenges and rewards they bring. Joanna shared some tips and recommendations, and I appreciated her friendly advice.

As our conversation naturally ended, we exchanged a friendly nod, each of us continuing on our way.

"Good luck with your apartment, Quinn," Joanna said with a parting smile.

"Thanks," I said.

The car doors were unlocked, so I loaded everything inside. As I returned from pushing my cart back inside, I saw Harry coming down the sidewalk. He'd been to the Super Mart for some groceries. I helped him put his two bags in the car, and we went back to the restaurant.

Armed with cleaning supplies and a determined spirit, I stepped into the apartment above the garage. It was time to transform this neglected space into a place I could call home. The apartment had a musty odor, a testament to years of disuse. Dust clung to every surface, and cobwebs dangled from the corners of the ceiling. I had my work cut out for me, but I wasn't daunted. The promise of a fresh start filled me with energy.

I got to work. Hours passed in a blur as I carried out bags of trash, clearing out the remnants of the past. Dust rabbits—too big to be called bunnies—scattered like fugitives as I swept the floors. The screech of my mop against the faded linoleum was a symphony of progress. Each swipe of the cloth, each spray of cleaner, brought me closer to my vision of a revitalized space. The once-grimy kitchenette now gleamed under new fluorescent lights. The living area, once cluttered and forlorn, looked one hundred times better. It was as if the apartment itself appreciated the care I was pouring into it. Once everything was clean, I washed down the walls like my momma taught me and painted them a pale blue that looked almost white in the early morning light. It felt like walking into a room cut out of the sky and clouds.

Totally satisfied, I brought up all the furniture I'd found in the garage. It was just enough to fill up the room. I opened the windows to get a cross-draft, allowing the cool breeze to freshen the air and let in the soft murmur of the ocean and the distant sounds of seagulls. It was the perfect soundtrack for renewal. Still, I put on a little music, using the tiny speaker tethered to my phone, as I stocked the kitchen cabinets, snagging a few pots, some plates, silverware, and glassware from the Shack until I could buy some down the road.

There wasn't much room in the bedroom with a queen-size bed in the middle of the floor, so I stashed all my gear in the closet and put my clothes in the chest of drawers. As I worked, I could see the transformation taking place around me and felt it taking place inside me. The apartment was slowly shedding its neglected past and embracing a brighter future, reflecting who I was becoming. I'd been a nomad since I was seventeen, and for the past three years, I'd crashed in fine hotels and magnificent villas with anywhere between nine and eleven other guys. This was my first place of my own, and it felt like a first-rate win.

I invited Harry over after work, and we stood back to admire my handiwork. He was as impressed as I was. The transformation was remarkable. What was once a forgotten and neglected space had become clean, bright, and welcoming. Harry even brought me a plant as a housewarming gift—a big fig leaf that was almost too large for the corner I put it in. I was grinning like a loon, relishing the sense of accomplishment and the quiet content that filled me.

Situated in my little abode, I spent a lot of time at the Shack. The lunch rush was a beast that kept the two of us hopping. I don't know how he managed it all by himself. Most of our patrons were local shop owners and their employees who sought quick meals—burgers and battered fish sandwiches and baskets of crisply fried shrimp and calamari rings. Every day, Harry handled the kitchen, and my role was to ensure everything else ran smoothly. I bussed the few tables we had, cleared away empty plates, wiped down surfaces, and washed pots and baskets in the back. The chatter of the lunch crowd provided a lively backdrop as I went about my tasks.

The front was a different kind of busy than the kitchen, but I didn't mind it. There was satisfaction in keeping everything neat and orderly, the floor clean. As I navigated the hustle and bustle, a familiar face walked through the door. It was Joanna, and I couldn't help but smile as she approached me.

"Hey there, Quinn," she greeted me with a friendly smile.

"Joanna, it's good to see you again," I replied, genuinely pleased by her presence. I walked her the short distance to the counter where Harry waited to take orders. His brows rose in surprise. She perused the menu on the chalkboard behind me while I stood with her, grinning like a buffoon.

"I'll have the Deluxe Fish Sandwich, please," she said, and Harry nodded. "Great choice. Would you like it with fries and slaw?"

She nodded. "Yes, please."

"Coming right up." As she turned to find a table to wait, I whispered to Harry, "On me, Harry."

"Yeah, Kid. I got 'cha."

When I brought her order over to her, Joanna raised an eyebrow, clearly surprised.

"Oh, Quinn, you don't have to do that."

I shook my head. "Consider it a thank you for your help and advice."

She giggled a bit, her eyes sparkling with gratitude. "Well, in that case, thank you, Quinn. I appreciate it."

She left with her lunch, probably taking it back to the bank to eat, and I could hear Harry chuckling behind the counter. I returned to work, catching up on the slack I'd created. I wasn't looking for a girlfriend at the moment, considering I was just starting to get some direction in my life, but she was nice and easy to talk to. Besides, I hadn't met many other people besides our customers, and it was nice to have a friend amidst the chaos.

CHAPTER
SEVEN

It was way cool to live so close to work and the ocean.

Most mornings, I could wake up when the first rays of the sun painted the horizon in hues of orange and pink. I'd grab my surfboard and make my way down to the ocean, feeling a familiar excitement that never failed to stir my soul. Securing the leash around my ankle, I'd run out into the water, relishing the tug of the ocean calling me home. The sound of the waves as they careened in, picking up speed just beyond the break and crashing against the shore, was irresistible. I took a deep breath, savoring the scent of saltwater and the tang of the sea breeze. With practiced ease, I hopped onto my board, the gentle lapping of the waves inviting me deeper, and began to paddle out. The surfboard felt like an extension of myself as I moved past the breakers, the world reduced to the rhythm of my breath and the rise and fall of the swell.

I sat astride my board, waiting for the perfect wave, anticipation electric in the air. The sun kissed the water's surface as I spotted it—a sleek, rolling wave that promised a thrilling ride. With a burst of energy, I paddled hard, feeling the wave lift me, the sheer power of nature propelling me forward. I popped up onto my feet, the board gliding smoothly beneath me. Time seemed to slow as I rode the crest of the wave, the world a blur of water, sun, and sky. It was a dance between me and nature, a connection that transcended words. As the wave eventually lost its momentum and I rode it to shore, I couldn't help but smile. Living by the ocean, with work steps away and the waves always within reach, was like therapy for my soul.

I'd stay out a couple of hours each morning before work, then head back to the apartment to shower and get myself ready to help Harry—I didn't really think of it as work. By the time I'd come in, the Shack would be buzzing with the regulars, sitting around, reading the papers, drinking coffee, and chitchatting with Harry. Then, the lunch rush would slam us. After that, it would be pretty slow, just a trickle of customers flowing in and out. Harry would fill the lull with long-winded monologues, stories, and anecdotes from when he was still a Marine and deployed overseas. His tales seemed to have a life of their own, a thread that wove its way through the chaos and the quiet, entertaining me while sharing a lesson or a moral by the end of my day.

We worked well together, side by side. Harry's voice carried over the sounds of sizzling pans and clinking dishes. At first, his precise, disciplined manner and gruff commands reminded me of my father, a man whose harsh and insensitive demeanor had left its mark on my childhood. He'd taught me to anticipate what needed doing before he could whip out with a fist or a belt and start pummeling me. Alvin D.J. Lawler was the sole reason I'd left home at seventeen and had never once returned, not even to check on my momma. She'd made our beds, and I wasn't one to lie in them.

But as I got to know Harry, it became apparent that he was nothing like my father. His stories weren't tales of harsh discipline and cold authority; they were stories of camaraderie, resilience, and the human side of military life. Between taking orders, serving dishes, and clearing tables, I found myself drawn into Harry's stories and his world. He told me about being a Black man in the military, the challenges he faced, and the bonds he formed with his fellow Marines. His words were filled with respect and admiration for the men and women he had served with, and it was clear that those experiences had shaped him into the person he was today. His stories were like windows into a world I had never known, a world of sacrifice and honor. It was a stark contrast to spending time with my father, a man who had never shown me kindness or understanding.

As the days turned to weeks and more than a month had passed, I realized that Harry had become more than just my boss; he'd also become more than just a friend. His willingness to share his experiences and his genuine concern for the well-being of those around him spoke volumes about his character. And he'd become a lifeline, a reminder that not all authority figures were like my father and that there were people in the world who valued compassion and empathy.

The lunch rush was in full swing at the Seafood Shack, and I was busy juggling orders and ensuring everything ran smoothly.

If this was considered slow after the summer season, I couldn't imagine what I was in for come summer. But today I was amped up for a different reason. I had a plan in mind—one that made my heart race with nervous anticipation. I hadn't seen Joanna in a couple of days, though I looked for her every day. As I hustled between the dining area and the kitchen, I couldn't help but steal glances at the door, waiting for her to show up. She had become a familiar and welcome presence in my life, and today, I intended to ask her out.

When the bell above the door jingled, and she stepped inside, her warm smile and kind eyes shining, I couldn't help but feel a flutter of excitement mixed with a touch of nerves.

"Hey, Joanna, good to see you again," I greeted her as she approached the counter.

"Hey, Quinn," she replied, her smile brightening. "It's always nice to be here."

I took her order on Harry's little notepad and handed it to him. He gave a sly smile since he was standing right there. I led her off to the side, out of the way of other customers trying to get their orders in, and cleared my throat, feeling a rush of nerves.

"Joanna," I began, trying to keep my tone steady, "I was wondering if you'd be interested in going out with me sometime."

She paused, her eyes locking onto mine, and I couldn't help but hold my breath in anticipation. After a moment that felt like an eternity, her smile widened, and she nodded. "I'd love to, Quinn."

Relief and joy washed over me, and I couldn't help but return her smile with one of my own. "Great. How about Friday night?"

She thought about it for a moment, probably mentally going over her schedule, a contemplative expression on her face. "Friday works for me. Where do you have in mind?"

I leaned in slightly, my voice softening. "I don't know. I'm new around here. Where would you like to go or do?"

"Let me think about it, and I'll let you know tomorrow." I nodded, just happy that she agreed to go out with me. I could hardly contain my excitement. As the lunch rush continued around us, our conversation flowed effortlessly, filled with the promise of a date to come. It was a moment of connection and anticipation, one that left me with a newfound sense of hope and happiness.

I stood in front of the mirror, trying to tame my unruly, sun-bleached hair with a palmful of gel. Tonight was the night I'd been looking forward to, but it also brought a swirl of emotions I couldn't ignore. Joanna had agreed to go out with me, and that alone sent a warm rush of happiness through my veins. She was the kind of girl who had her life together—a stable job, probably a clear road map for the future.

On the other hand, I was a hot mess, not entirely sure where I was headed, and truth be told, maybe I shouldn't be dragging her into my whirlpool of uncertainty. What did I have to offer Joanna, or anyone, aside from a surfboard and a bag full of insecurities? I took a deep breath, trying to shake off the doubts that threatened to cloud my excitement. She'd agreed to this date because she wanted to spend time with me, right? Maybe she saw something in me that I couldn't quite see in myself at the moment.

I hurriedly put on the clothes I'd picked out for the evening: a blue silk designer pullover, a pair of soft charcoal jeans with a few strategic rips—they looked shredded on purpose—and the sneakers I'd set out. Glancing at the clock, I realized it was almost time to head out. I met my reflection in the mirror with a grin and grabbed my keys, and Harry's car keys.

"Quinn, my friend," I said, locking the apartment door behind me, "you might be a hot mess, but sometimes, that's exactly what makes life interesting."

I settled into the driver's seat and fought with the adjustments to accommodate my shorter legs and arms. Harry was at least three, four, maybe five inches taller than me, and I was six-one. I felt like a kid climbing behind the wheel after him. If I stayed here, I was going to need a car, something a little fresher than Harry's sedan, but for now, it was going to do nicely. The engine turned over and hummed with a familiar, reassuring growl, and I saw that the tank was full. Harry kept this baby in good shape, even if it was pushing a decade. It was reliable, just like him.

As I navigated the streets on my way to pick up Joanna, my mind was a whirlwind of thoughts. What was she thinking about this whole situation? Her world was filled with balance sheets and spreadsheets, and she probably had the evening all planned out for us. Me? I was just going with the flow, happy to be out and having some fun. We're just going to have a good time. I took a deep breath, feeling the freedom of being behind the wheel, and gunned it.

I arrived at the bank a little early, and I waited in the car, my stomach doing somersaults. When she finally stepped out of the bank, my breath caught. She was a vision with a smile that could outshine the California sun. She waved at me, and I flashed a grin that I hoped came off as charming rather than too eager.

"Hey, Quinn," she greeted me, her voice warm and inviting.

"Hey, what's up? How've you been?" I asked, getting out of the car to open the door for her.

"Good. You?"

"I'm good. Where're we going? Point me in the right direction."

"We can walk over to Patty's. It's a nice place. A diner where we can sit, eat, and, you know, talk. They don't rush you. Unless you want to go to a fancy restaurant. Leona's Italian is a little ways out."

"I'm with you, babe. Wherever you want to go."

She laughed, and I reached over to help her get out of the seatbelt.

"You're going to fix my seatbelt all evening?" she asked, bursting out laughing. It was like music to my ears—genuine, if I had to describe it, and I joined her.

"It depends. You might get the hang of it before long. You have to hold it like this," I said, showing her. She took it from me and hooked it without any trouble, then looked at me with her eyebrows practically meeting her hairline, though she was still smiling.

"I don't know how you did that so easily. I always have trouble when I'm in that seat," I defended myself.

We parked in the city lot and walked across the street to Patty's Diner a few blocks over. We took a table off to the side. The conversation flowed effortlessly. We shared stories about our lives, and I found myself captivated by Joanna's genuine personality. She had this way of making me feel comfortable like I could be myself without any pretense. She didn't believe me when I told her that I surfed professionally for the past three years until I pulled out my social media and showed her all the pictures. Then she looked at me, all agog, like I was some celebrity or something. I felt flattered for a minute, but I liked it better when she didn't know about my surfing. I was just a regular person then.

Over burgers and shakes, our chatter picked up, ranging from favorite surf spots to the latest film releases. Joanna had a deep love for classic cinema, while I leaned more toward action flicks. Yet, there was plenty of time and room to find some common ground. Leaving the diner, we strolled towards the movie theater. I kinda liked the fact that most everything was within walking distance. I'd grown up in a small coastal town just like this in Northern California, and it all felt familiar.

The sun had dipped below the horizon, leaving the darkening sky streaked with slashes of orange and pink, and a cool breeze blew in from the ocean. Joanna slipped her arm through mine, and I couldn't help but smile and give her arm a squeeze against my side. We pulled up to Joanna's apartment building, the soft glow of the streetlights casting a warm ambiance on the sidewalk. The evening had been a mix of laughter, shared stories, and the simple pleasure of each other's company. As I parked the car and turned off the engine, I turned to Joanna with a big smile.

"I had a great time tonight."

She returned the smile, her eyes shining. "Me too, Quinn. Thanks for a wonderful evening."

I leaned back in the driver's seat, my fingers drumming lightly on the steering wheel. "We should do this again sometime, you know? Maybe catch a different movie or try out that new café down the street. Maybe you can even come hang out with me at the beach sometime."

Joanna's nod was filled with warmth and agreement. "I'd like that, Quinn. Will you teach me to surf?"

"Absolutely. I even have a couple of boards you can try out."

"Sounds like fun."

We exchanged numbers, and then we lingered a moment longer. I wanted to hold her, maybe give her a kiss, but I was unsure how she would respond. We'd been casual all evening, and though I thought it was, like, perfect, maybe she didn't see me the same way. Still, she agreed to hang out with me again, and I climbed out of the car to open the door for her. As she stepped out onto the sidewalk, her eyes locked with mine, giving me goosebumps, and I thought, yeah, there was no way she wasn't at least a little bit into me. I took her hand and walked her to the entrance of her building, and she hugged me, letting me feel her in my arms, and a sweet goodnight kiss. It made me feel like I was sixteen again with my first crush. I wasn't ready to let her go, but she stepped out of the circle of my arm, gave me another smile, and waved goodbye before disappearing inside. I stood there a moment, getting all the feels and staring into the night before I pulled myself together and went back to the car.

Back behind the wheel, I decided that I liked the feel of her in my arms and the feel of her lips against mine, and I needed her practical mind and sense of humor. I felt a sense of contentment settle over me. I couldn't wait to see her again.

CHAPTER
EIGHT

It was starting to feel like things were shaking out pretty well for me.

The tides of my life had turned here in this little in-between town of San Nobel. I'd moved out of the Cloverleaf Motel almost a month ago and was vibing happily on Harry's ex-wife's studio apartment above the garage. Each day was less about counting time and more about making time count. I had settled into a rhythm, one not dictated by competition schedules or sponsor demands, but by the simple cadence of getting up, surf a little, and go to work. Rinse and repeat. You know, daily life. Morning runs along the shoreline weren't for training; they were meditations, where each stride on the damp sand was a step away from who I used to be toward who I was becoming.

The Shack had become my dojo, the grill my sensei. Each order was a lesson in patience; each satisfied customer was a nod to my growing competence. I was crafting more than meals; I was crafting a new self, one that could find as much value in steady work as in the thrill of victory.

My evenings were once filled with the noise of revelry, but

now they were quieter, marked by the gentle clatter of cutlery as I prepped for the next day and the soft laughter of beach-goers winding down their day. And when Joanna and I hung out, her playful banter was a melody that made the simplest moments feel like scenes from a life I was only starting to appreciate.

The mirror next to the front door of my little apartment is no longer a reminder of a fall from grace. It now reflected a face that had lost the hollowness of rejection and lost opportunities. My hands, rough from work, were strong—capable of rebuilding a life I once thought was beyond repair. I'd regained the ten pounds I'd lost during my bout of depression. As I sat on the orange futon covered by a navy and baby blue spread, its worn fabric a testament to endurance, I realized I was experiencing a sense of peace that was entirely new to me. This was not the erratic peace brokered with the highs of past victories or lows of defeat; this was the peace of self-acceptance, of small triumphs that, day by day, were reconstructing the identity of Quinn Anthony Lawler—not the surfer legend, but the man of simple pleasures and honest work. I was in no rush to end my days, no desire to hasten my nights. For the first time in a long while, I was in step with time, not racing against it. Yeah, things were definitely starting to shake out pretty well.

Dawn broke like a raw egg over the horizon, and I was out front of the Shack, my feet buried in the cool sand, entranced with the colors spilling out across the sky—streaks of pink and orange bleeding into blue. I didn't go for my morning Zen. Instead of getting up at first light to watch the new day awaken, I was on a mission, and it was fortunate for me that my commute to work was like two minutes long.

This morning, I was going to surprise Harry…and make my job a little easier. I unlocked the door, the metallic click echoing like some starting pistol, and went inside, locking the door behind me. Harry is usually here long before I come down. He usually opened up for a few regulars who come in for coffee, breakfast sandwiches, and some company, but today, I beat him here. I had a plan, a mission. I was going to get the back organized. I heaved open the wooden shutters to air the place out. The view outside was beautiful and pristine. The first rays of the sun were shy, just barely kissing the edge of the water, as the ocean huffed in and out, and the salty, briny breeze blew in through the window, swirling around and clearing out the odors of yesterday's fried fish.

A part of me, the old part, still couldn't believe my days now started with wiping out coffee pots after getting wiped out on the waves, and I laughed at my own jokes. I ground the coffee beans, and the machine whirred loudly—a sound that had become as comforting as any old tune. It's funny how the little things become your anchors. As the Shack started to smell less like the ocean and more like a cafe, I got to work. I made a space for the pots and pans, organized the cabinets so things were within easy reach, and I got to work in the pantry. I don't know how he knew what was where or how much he had. Every time I had to go in there, it took me at least twenty minutes to find something. When Harry came in at seven-thirty, he started grinning like someone had popped a surprise party for him.

"Hey, morning Quinn. What's all this?"

"Hmmm? You're late this morning, Boss. Good thing I'm here to get things started."

"Yeah, looks like it. Thanks. I smell coffee."

"Yeah, it's ready," I said, grinning from ear to ear. "Let me get you a cup."

We didn't have a lot of time for him to see everything I'd done, but I knew he'd appreciate the pantry more than anything. The bell above the door kept a steady tinkling sound as the regulars shuffled in and out.

"Morning, Harry, Quinn," greeted Mr. Peterson, his voice as craggy as the rocks lining the shore. He was usually one of the earliest to arrive, his morning paper tucked under his arm, and Harry always had his coffee ready, black with a single spoon of sugar.

"Yo, Pete," I nod, setting his mug on the table in front of him. "Waves are lookin' real rad out there today, huh?"

He grunted in agreement, glancing up at me with his pale blue eyes, unfolding the paper with a crackle that competes with the breaking waves outside. He doesn't talk much, but his grunt and nod are like some ancient seal of approval. Other regulars trickled in, a parade of familiar faces. Rosie rushes in with her twin boys, who've got energy like they've got springs for legs, bouncing around while she orders a latte, three croissant sandwiches and two containers of chocolate milk. She always comes in early and gets her coffee and breakfast for her and the boys on her way to drop them off at daycare.

"Keeping' you on your toes, huh?" I grin as I hand over the coffee and the bag with everything else inside. I barely manage to catch the small, errant hand aiming for a tip jar filled with sand dollars. I moved the jar back and put two individually wrapped cooking in his hand instead.

Rosie laughs, that full-bellied sound that reminds me of better days, "Always, Quinn. Always."

As the Shack fills up, the hum of conversation mixes with the seagulls squawking above. This joint, man, it's like the heartbeat of the beach. Most of the shop owners and their employees stop by sometime during the day—before opening, for lunch, and maybe for a quick pick-me-up in the afternoon. Lots of other people come in, keeping the shop humming all day, but I'm getting to know our regulars, and they make the day pleasant. Yeah, pleasant is a good word for it. I sling espressos and smoothies and crack jokes, and I'm not just the new guy, the surfer dude with the laid-back vibe, anymore; I'm part of the woodwork, part of their morning ritual. And that's... well, that's totally rad.

The bell over the door kept tinkling, and I kept moving, riding this new wave of life. It may be near the ocean, but it's got its own ebb and flow. And, for now, I'm pretty pumped up to be a part of it.

As the afternoon sun started throwing long shadows across the Shack's floorboards, Harry's voice cut through the haze of the late-season heat, "Alright, Kid, let's get this inventory done."

I let him go first. I know he hadn't seen the pantry because he'd been sending me back there all morning. I followed, hoping to get a look at his face when he saw the back shelves all neat and organized. It's a different kind of lineup than I'm used to—cans of tomato sauce and stacks of napkins instead of waves. But it was worth it when Harry looked around, nodding, taking in every single item clearly displayed: everything in its place and a place for everything.

Harry's hands trembled and had I not been watching him, I might have missed it, but I could see how moved he was. He cleared his throat and rasped out a heartfelt, Thank You, Quinn.

"How else are we going to keep track of what we've got and what we need? It's not just about having enough; it's about smart ordering so we're not wasting cash or space," I repeated his words from yesterday when he told me we needed to do inventory. Looking at my handiwork, it looked like we had a whole lot of everything imaginable, but then, what did I know about outfitting a pantry?

"I just plan to keep it neat from now on, okay, Boss?"

"Yeah, Quinn. I'll try to keep it like this, too. Now, hand me that clipboard, will ya?" Harry said, his voice snapping us back to our task. I passed it over, watching him make meticulous notes. Harry treated the inventory like a sacred ritual. Every can, every box, every bag had its place, its purpose. It was about being prepared and knowing your arsenal, so when the lunch and dinner rushes hit, we were ready, and it all looked like a piece of cake to those waiting for their orders.

We started taking inventory at one end of the top shelf all the way to the bottom one. Then, we started on the chiller, counting all the refrigerated food items. It went smoothly as Harry could see how much of what he had, and I made room for things we were out of. As I stood there in the pantry with Harry, I couldn't help but draw a line between this and my days on the circuit. We were knee-deep in cans of tomatoes and sacks of flour, ticking off items for the next delivery. It was a far cry from the sun, sand, and surf, but there was a rhythm to it, a method that reminded me of prepping for a competition. I started to see the parallels. Just like in surfing, where the flashy moves on the waves were backed by hours of practice, muscle memory, and knowing your gear inside out, here in the Shack's pantry, our behind-the-scenes prep was what made the service seamless. Harry caught me staring off into space, lost in thought.

"What's on your mind, Kid?"

"Just thinking about how all this," I gestured around the pantry, "is a lot like getting ready for a heat. The prep work nobody sees. It's what makes the difference between success and failure."

He nodded, his chocolate eyes lighting up with understanding. "Exactly. The show's only as good as the work you put in when nobody's watching."

As we continued the inventory, I couldn't shake the feeling of satisfaction. Something was grounding about it. Each item we checked off felt like a small victory, a step towards a bigger goal. It was a reminder that the best performances, whether in a surf competition or a bustling kitchen, were built on a foundation of unseen effort and dedication. In those moments, among the spices and canned goods, I found a new respect for the process, for the meticulous planning and preparation that made the Shack more than just a place to eat. It was a well-oiled machine, and I was a cog in something much larger than myself.

My ego and curiosity inflated a hundred times bigger, I asked, "Who's our main supplier for the fresh stuff?" Moving over by the produce, the scent of limes and cilantro mixed in the air. I wanted to know everything.

"Luciano's. They're local and family-owned. Fresh and fast —and our customers appreciate that. But you gotta watch 'em. They'll try to offload the near-turns if you don't keep an eye out," Harry explains, his eyes sharp.

I think back to the sponsors, always trying to slap their logos on my board, my life. I was always watching them, too. Deals that seemed good but had strings attached, waves that promised a ride but held a wipe-out. I get it, I think, this whole inventory thing—it's like choosing the right sponsor, picking the right wave. It's knowing what'll carry you through to the end of the competition or the end of the month. Man, I say aloud, though I didn't realize it, everything's relevant.

As we finish up, Harry slaps the clipboard down. "Good job today, Quinn. Thanks for all this," he says, waving his arm to encompass the pantry and getting us organized out there."

I can't help the grin that breaks across my face. Maybe it's not the winner's podium, but it feels pretty damn close.

When I left the Shack, the sun started to dip below the

horizon, painting the sky with a goodbye kiss of purples and oranges, and I realized I'd been there all day. The sun had started setting earlier in the evening, and customer traffic usually trickled off by five, but today had been exceptionally quiet, and had sped by so fast I didn't even realize I'd put in more than eight hours. Maybe,... I thought as I jogged up the stairs to my sanctuary, "Maybe it was a sign of times to come.

~

I flipped the sign on the door to Closed, locked it, and started sweeping and wiping down the tables and chairs. The Shack felt different in the silence like it was exhaling after holding its breath all day, and the cleanup went fast. Harry was in the back, probably cleaning the grill, so I was surprised when he came out to the counter and called me over.

"Grab a seat, Quinn. I think we've earned this," he says, his voice a little softer now that we don't have to shout over people's conversations. I pull a rickety chair up to a table as Harry brings over a couple of cold ones and two plates of grilled fish tacos, black beans and seasoned rice, the charred smell mingling with the salty evening air. It's nothing fancy, but damn, does it look like a feast.

"Cheers," he says, raising his bottle of beer. "And Happy Thanksgiving." I froze for a moment. Thanksgiving? Already? I hadn't realized how much time had passed.

I knocked mine against it, the clink a solid, real sound. "Happy Thanksgiving, Harry," I replied, and we both took long swallows, the beer cold and sharp down my throat.

We dig into the tacos, the fish flaking perfectly, and the calamari rings. Every bite was a reminder of the ocean steps away. I don't think I've had a better meal in any of the fancy restaurants I've ever eaten in. And sitting with Harry was so damn peaceful, just the sound of the waves and the occasional cry of a night bird to keep us company. Harry's usually a man of few words, but tonight, there's something like contemplation in his gaze as he looks out at the darkening water.

"You know, Quinn," he starts, and I can tell he's about to drop some of that grizzled wisdom he's full of, "life's a lot like surfing. You'll wipe out and get tossed around by the waves, but it's all about paddling back out there."

I nod because, hell, he's right. Not too long ago, I was floating, man, letting the current take me wherever, thinking maybe I'd sink. But here I am, paddling back out, finding my rhythm again.

"It's good, you know," I say, "feeling the board under my feet. Not literally, I mean... this," I gestured around the Shack, "feeling useful."

Harry looks at me, and there's a flash of something like pride in his eyes. "You're more than useful, Kid. You're essential."

Those words hit me like a fresh swell. It's like something Colin would say. He's the only other person who believed in me. He believed in all of us groms. I looked down at my plate and nodded.

"Thanks, man," I said, feeling a little choked up. Colin was gone, but Harry…, well, it seems like Harry was kinda like Colin. He must see something in me, too, and maybe this is all a new beginning. I've been so focused on surviving, on just making it through, that I didn't realize I was actually moving forward, that I was becoming a part of something. It's not just about making it to the next day anymore; it's about making those days count, finding those moments of joy in the simple things like a good beer, a perfect taco, and a quiet night with a person who's seen it all and is still standing.

The night settled around us like a blanket, and we sat inside the Shack, two dudes sharing a meal, not needing to say much. Because, like, yeah, life threw us both some lame breaks, but here we are, still riding the waves. And for the first time since I was canned, I'm stoked to see what's next.

CHAPTER NINE

The next day rolled in bright and clear, the kind of SoCal day that postcards are made of.

The sun was high, and the sky was this wild, endless blue that stretched out forever. Harry cut me loose early because he didn't expect a big lunch rush. Free for the day, I texted Joanna to see if she wanted to hang out after work. She said she had the day off and would meet me on the beach. I went back upstairs and got two boards. When I came back forty minutes later, I saw Joanna awkwardly wrestling with a wetsuit she'd rented from the surf shop further down on the beach. I tried not to laugh because, man, I've been there.

"Need a hand?" I call out as I jog over, two boards tucked under my arm.

She looks up, a smile fighting with the frustration on her face. "Only if you promise not to make fun of me."

"No promises," I say, but I kneeled to help her tug the stubborn neoprene over her knees.

Once she's finally suited up, we hit the waves—or, well, they pretty much hit us. I showed her how to mount her board in the water and how to paddle out.

"Keep your back arched, like you're trying to hold the sky up," I tell her, and she's a natural, sort of. She's got the spirit, if not the balance, but that comes with time. And hell, it's funny to watch her wipe out and come up spitting seawater and laughter. We spend the rest of the afternoon chasing waves, and I show her the ropes, teaching her how to read the water.

"See that swell there? That's yours. Paddle hard now," I urge, and she paddles like she's trying to outrun a shark, and for a second, she's up, actually up, before the ocean takes her back. But the grin on her face when she surfaces is brighter than the sun overhead.

"Again!" she demands, and who am I to argue with that kind of stoke?

Between the attempts and the actual surfing, we talk—about everything and nothing. The chatter's easy, and it's cool to have someone just vibing with the day, with the surf, with me. We're not trying to unpack our life stories or anything; we're just there, in the moment, and it's a good place to be. Every now and then, I catch her watching me with this thoughtful look, like she's figuring something out, but then she's laughing again, and I decide it's not the day to dive deep into whatever that's about.

As the afternoon sun began to sink behind the horizon, our shadows grew long on the wet sand, and we were just a couple of friends sharing the last waves while the sky was throwing down shades of pink and orange. It was a blast, the kind of simple fun I haven't had in ages, the kind where you forget about competing and training and keeping your focus. We were both getting better at this—her with learning to surf and me with…I don't know, life maybe? There's a rhythm to it all, and I'm finally catching the beat.

CHAPTER
TEN

The next afternoon, Harry tossed me the keys to the Shack with a clink of trust.

"Gotta head out for a check-up with the doctor. You got this, Quinn?"

I grasp the keys, feeling their cold weight and sharp edges.

"Got it, Harry. Go get that clean bill of health, yeah?"

He grins, a crack in his usual stoic facade. "Don't burn down the place, Kid."

As soon as he's gone, the place feels different—it's mine to run, even if just for a few hours. I stand behind the counter, surveying my domain with my hands on my hips, when the door swings open. It's just Mr. Jacobsen, a retiree with a love for our spicy shrimp tacos and stories from his sailing days that could fill a dozen books. He's got this wind-worn face that's always smiling, and he never misses a chance to say, "Make it extra hot, boy! I need to feel alive!"

I chuckle and get to work, prepping his order while he regales me with a tale of a storm off the Cape of Good Hope. I told him I'd been there before, and his laughter had filled the Shack.

Now, he always has stories to tell me about his time there, and I feel a swell of pride delivering his tacos with an extra side of freshly chopped jalapeños.

A steady stream of locals and tourists, each with their own quirks, stop in. I meet a pair of surfer girls, Tia and Lani, who debate the best surf spots like they're discussing world peace. They're local and out doing some Christmas shopping. They order smoothies, and as the blender whirs, the three of us chitchat. They leave, promising to come back with friends. Then there's a hiccup—a delivery guy shows up with more fish than we ordered.

"Where do you want it, dude?" he asks, looking at the invoice and then at me.

I checked our order log, and my heart is racing, but it's an error on their end, not ours.

"We can't take all this, man. Check the slip again," I tell him.

He scratches his head, the phone pressed to his ear, and after a brief conversation, he hauls half of it back. Crisis averted, and I'm buzzing with the thrill of handling it solo. The afternoon isn't all smooth waves though. A new customer, a lady with a sharp tongue and a designer handbag, makes a fuss about the wait time. "I've been standing here for ten minutes!" she snaps, checking her watch like it's a ticking bomb. I apologize, feeling the heat rise, and focus on her order—a simple fish sandwich, making sure it's the best damn fish sandwich we've ever served. When I set it in front of her, she's still fuming, but after a bite, her eyes soften. "Well, this is delightful," she admits, and I mentally pat myself on the back.

I'm amped. The Shack is my ship, and I'm steering her through choppy waters, feeling more in command with every order I take and every problem I solve. When Harry returns a few hours later, just before dark, he finds me wiping down the counters, the Shack still standing, the customers happy. "So, no fires then?" he asks, a twinkle in his eye.

"Smooth sailing, Harry. And the Shack's all shipshape," I say with a grin.

He claps my shoulder, and I think, yeah, I can do this. I can manage more than just a surfboard. For the first time in a long while, I'm not just waiting for the next wave—I'm already riding it.

The Shack had its moods, you know, and that day, it was almost contemplative, like it knew when to hush the usual clatter and chatter and give some space to the weightier silences.

The late afternoon sun cast a warm glow over the Shack, but the air carried a chill that said the day and the year was winding down. Harry was behind the counter, cleaning up the grill with methodical strokes, the way a soldier might clean his rifle—habitual, almost meditative. I'd just finished wiping down all of the tables and was perched on one of the stools, nursing a soda, the fizz of it a sharp contrast to the somber mood that had settled over us. Then Harry came over and leaned over on the counter, resting on both elbows. The lines on his face were more pronounced in the orange wash of the setting sun coming through the front door and windows. It felt like the day had taken a deep breath, holding it in, bracing itself. He started talking, his voice a low rumble, barely above the hum of the distant waves.

"I have a son, you know?" He said, turning to look at me. I said nothing because it didn't really feel like he was asking me a question. "His name is Carson," he began, the pain evident in his voice as if each word was being coaxed from a place deep and scarred. "Carson Harrison Dawes. He had a smile that could light up the darkest room, and Sylvia, his mom...well, she took him away when he was just a little guy. maybe six or close to it. That was fifteen years ago."

I paused, my soda sitting on my thigh, and listened.

"She couldn't handle being the wife of a Marine, you know. Raising our child by herself because I was always being deployed somewhere away from them for months, sometimes a year or more at a time. And I wasn't...I wasn't an easy man to be with when I was home. Not with the anger, the back all messed up from a bad drop. I couldn't be the Marine I was, and I couldn't be the husband or dad they needed. So she left."

There was a clink as he set a glass down behind the counter a little too hard. His eyes weren't on me; they were somewhere far off, riding waves of a past he usually kept anchored deep.

"I don't know where they went. I don't know where they are now. I haven't heard a word in all these years. Carson would be 'bout your age now, I guess. Twenty-one. You about that age, right?"

I nodded. "Twenty-three on the twentieth." I didn't know what else to say. What could I say? So, I just went over and leaned beside him, on the opposite side of the counter, offering silence as a space for his story.

"A couple of weeks, Huh? You remind me of him...you know, of who I think he'd be now. Who I hope he'd be."

I felt that—a connection, not just between two guys working a shack, but between two souls adrift, finding some common current in this wide, wild ocean of life. The silence stretched long and thin like the years Harry had gone without his boy, and I felt his pain.

"Yeah," I finally said, my voice barely a whisper, "I get it. The whole 'missing pieces' thing."

Harry gave a nod, as if acknowledging the truth that we both lived with. A single nod that said, "I know you do."

"You know something, Harry," I said, my mouth working before my brain got in gear. "for years, I wished my momma would've finally gotten up and left my old man... but she never did. She just put up with him year after year, even though he had this way of making everyone around him feel this small," I said, pinching my fingers until they almost touched. "We were dirt poor, but it wasn't because we didn't strive, you know. My father worked every day of his life, but it didn't make ends meet. And I guess that made him hard, as hard as they come. No room for error, no patience for dreams." I could still feel the sting of his words, barbed and cold, telling me I'd never amount to anything.

"So, I bailed the minute I could, an old, battered surfboard under my arm, heart pounding with this crazy idea that maybe, just maybe, I could ride waves to a better life." I let out a chuckle, the sound bitter against the quiet of the Shack. "And for a while, it worked, you know? I won second place at this amateur gig right outta high school. I didn't even stick around to get my diploma. The school mailed it to my momma sometime after I left. I hit the amateur circuit, lived out of a van with a bunch of other guys, chased the waves, and lived off whatever I won."

Harry's eyes were wide, reflecting a story he hadn't expected. "Quinn, I had no idea."

"Yeah, I get it. But then I met the guys. Josh Brenner, Sean Hargrove, Colin Mitchell. Look 'em up. They're the best there is, and it was a fluke, really. I don't even know what they were doing at that funky little amateur challenge up the coast from here, but Colin saw something in me. He was like... not just a mentor but the big brother I never had, and he believed in me. He pushed me to go pro. Those guys, they were like... nah, they were family for most of us. And, Dude, those three years with them were everything I could have imagined. Traveling, competing... winning. For a while there, I was somebody." The memories flooded in—the bright sun, the taste of salt on my lips, the cheer of the crowd. "For a few golden years, I'd had it all. "

Harry's brow rose, his interest piqued as he wiped down a glass. "You were a pro?" he asked, the surprise in his voice mirroring the surprise I felt when the team fell apart.

"Yeah. But it's like building a castle on sand, right? One big wipe-out, both in the waves and with my choices... and it all comes crashing down." There was a heaviness in my chest, a surfboard's weight of regret, but Harry reached over, giving my shoulder a squeeze that said more than words could.

"Life's a rogue wave, Quinn. It knocks you down when you least expect it." We shared a look, and I knew he got it—really got it. "But you know what?" Harry added, his voice gruff but not unkind. "You're paddling back out. That's what counts."

After a long minute, he asked, "So, your family, Quinn," Harry began, his voice careful, like he was stepping through a minefield, "Do you ever talk to 'em?" And there it was, the question that always seemed to hover in the air like a bad smell. I shook my head, a small movement that felt like I was shaking off a heavy weight.

"Nah, Harry. We're about as close as the sun and the moon—technically related but worlds apart."

He stopped scrubbing, the silence stretching between us, expectant. I traced the rim of the soda can with my fingertips, the metal shark but slick. "When I got second place in my first real competition, it was like a slap in the face to him, you know? Proving him wrong. Going pro and sending my momma money, sometimes my entire check was another blow to his ego. I could give her a couple thousand dollars and not miss a beat." I let out a chuckle, though there was no real humor in it.

"I surfed with them for three years. But then the shark attack happened last May, down in San Diego, while they were on vacation. It was unbelievable. Colin was killed, Josh was messed up, and all of our sponsorships dried up." I paused, my hand automatically reaching for the necklace I wore, a shark tooth talisman from those days.

"And what?" Harry prompted, leaning in, the glass forgotten.

"And Josh came back in September to root for the team and all that, but they cut us loose. Just like that," I said, snapping my fingers. The snap echoed, a stark reminder of how quickly life could flip. "They handed us severance checks in plain envelopes that felt like... I don't know, like tombstones marking the death of our dreams."

Harry nodded, a man who understood loss all too well. "Must've been tough," he said, his voice carrying the weight of empathy.

"The toughest part wasn't just losing out on the surfing; it was feeling betrayed, you know?" I leaned forward, finding solace in sharing. "They went back to Australia. Josh's family is like *God-awful* rich, and Sean made a lot of money on the circuit. They went back home to the lap of luxury. I wasn't so lucky. I ended up at the Cloverleaf fucking motel." I glanced up. I think that was the first curse word I'd ever uttered in front of him. But he didn't say anything, still looking off into the distance. "But, you know, looking back, I guess I get it. The team was gushing money from what I can understand. The money makers, Josh, Sean, and Colin were out. Vince, Jeff, and Marc were never in the same league as them, but they were good. They could be counted on to bring in steady money, and the rest of us were wildcards. Me and Lloyd, Joey, Jordan, popped big checks here and there, but we weren't steady. So, I guess there was no other way. It was a hard pill to swallow, but I didn't come to realize it wasn't just me who'd lost something—I wasn't the only one hurtin'."

I could see Harry's mind turning over the pieces of my story, maybe even seeing parallels with his own, but his eyes were wide, his mouth open, reflecting on a story he hadn't expected. "Quinn, I had no idea…."

"I know," I said. "Even in my first year with them, we were tearing up the pro circuit, hitting all the big spots. Australia, Brazil, and South Africa. South Africa was my favorite place, that and the south of France. Anyway, we'd all got a break after a grueling six months on tour after they hit big in Biarritz. They gave us three weeks off, and most of us either went home or just chilled in France. Me and a few buddies on the team stayed in there, chilling out in a Villa that belonged to a friend of a friend of Josh. The six of us hanging out in France, feeling like a bunch of kids let out of school." I chuckled. That had been a blast, but it didn't make the heaviness in my chest go away.

"That's a hell of a story, Quinn," Harry said finally. "But it ain't over yet. You've got more chapters to write."

I looked at him, really looked, and saw not just my boss or the guy who gave me a chance when I was down and out. I saw a friend.

"Yeah," I replied, feeling the first real spark of something that felt like hope. "Yeah, maybe I do. I still don't know what I want to do. Some days, I want to try again. It's expensive, you know, paying the fees, catching flights to chase the tourneys, hotels, all of that, but sometimes one winner's purse can cover a few months, and you get noticed. Sponsors come out of the woodwork to snap you up. We had some of the biggest sponsors in the industry because Josh, Sean, and Colin won more than half the challenges they entered," I admitted, my gaze drifting out to the horizon. "Other times, though, being here, grounded in a good way, finding a new rhythm—it's given me time and space to figure out what else is out there for me. My father used to tell me I'd never amount to anything. I got the chance to prove him wrong then. I still want to."

Harry grabbed my shoulder, his grip firm and reassuring. "Don't you believe him, Quinn. You've got to get him out of your head and lead your own life. Not going around trying to prove yourself to people who say stupid things." And in that shared silence, with the ocean whispering its endless stories, I felt the last of my resentment toward Josh and Sean ebb away. They hadn't screwed me over. They'd shown me a better life than I had at the time, but it wasn't the only way to a good life. Deep down, I still had hoped that I could make it back to pro surfing, but I knew it might not happen the way I envisioned it. Besides, to do it the only way I knew how, I would need a lot more money than what was currently in my bank account.

CHAPTER
ELEVEN

Have you ever, you know, like sometimes, spoke your hopes and dreams aloud, hoping that the universe heard you?.

And then it sent the very thing you wanted most your way—even if it's not the best thing for you or the right time for it? Well, the holidays were over, and Karma turned its sights on me one afternoon. The Shack had been quiet most of the day, but a group of customers came in together. Harry took care of them while I stacked up the clean pots on the wire rack I'd ordered and set up so Harry wouldn't have to dig around in the cabinets for a fresh pot every time. I'd laid my iPhone on the prep counter, which I seldom did, usually keeping it in my back pocket so I wouldn't misplace it or let it get knocked around and broken. However, a sound I hadn't heard in months pealed loud and clear, and the phone skittered across the stainless-steel countertop from the vibration. It kinda threw me off, what with me being so wrapped up in my new normal—waves, work, repeat—that that particular ringtone jarred me.

Harry, with a chuckle as he manned the grill, threw a teasing glance at me. "What, your secret admirers finally tracked you down?"

"Nah, probably someone who knows my car's warranty is about to expire," I joked. Wiping my hands on the damp, stained apron tied around my waist, I grabbed the phone. "Quinn here," I answered, my voice a stranger to my ears. The line crackled, then exploded with life.

"Quinn? Dude, it's Jordan." The voice on the other end of the line was familiar but somehow felt distant, like a faded photo of something once vibrant. My chest tightened at the sound, a mix of relief and unease washing over me. It had been months since we'd spoken, and hearing him now felt like a lifeline to a past I wasn't sure I wanted to revisit.

"Jordan? No way, man." I tried to keep my tone light, but I could feel the old camaraderie tugging at me. "Been a while. How've you been?"

"Better now that I've got you on the line," he said, laughing. His voice was as I remembered—warm, laid-back, always a hint of mischief. "Thought maybe you'd fallen off the face of the earth or something. I've been trying to get ahold of you. You know how it is. Life gets in the way."

I leaned back against the wall, trying to ignore the sudden rush of memories. "Yeah, tell me about it. I've been… busy." The word felt like a lie, even though it wasn't. Busy didn't begin to cover the mess I'd been sorting through, the rebuilding, the constant push and pull of trying to find myself again. "Sorry, I've been off the grid. Just had to get my head straight."

"I get it, man," Jordan said, his voice softening. "Things

have been crazy all around. I'm just glad to hear your voice. You sound… different. Good different."

I chuckled, though it felt forced. "Yeah, I guess. Trying to keep my feet on the ground, you know? What about you? How's everything going on your end?"

Jordan hesitated, and I could almost see him on the other side of the call, running a hand through his dreadlocks, searching for the right words. "It's been a wild ride, Q. You know how it goes. Still surfing, still grinding. Family's good, mostly. Mom's always worried, but that's nothing new. And the circuit… it's been rough without you. Not gonna lie."

The circuit. The team. That part of my life felt like another world, one I'd been trying to bury but couldn't quite let go of. "I miss it sometimes," I admitted, the words surprising me. "Not just the competitions but, you know, the guys. You, Gray, the whole crew."

"Same here, bro. It's not the same without you." Jordan's voice carried a weight that told me he meant every word. "Which is why I'm calling. Look, I know you're probably up to your eyeballs in… whatever you're doing now, but I've got an opportunity. And I think it's something you need to hear."

I felt my heart kick up a notch, anticipation curling around my thoughts. "Yeah? What's up?"

"The Aloha Challenge," he said, and I could hear the smile in his voice, like he knew he was dropping a bomb. "Hawaii's North Shore. It's happening, Quinn. And I want you there. With me."

My mind instantly flashed to the iconic waves, the rush of

the competition, the roar of the crowd. "That's huge, man. But I don't know, Jordan. I'm not sure I'm ready for all that. I've got a lot going on here."

"Come on, Q. Don't give me that," Jordan said, his tone somewhere between a plea and a challenge. "This is us. You and me. We've done crazier shit than this. I know things went south before, but we've got a chance to make things right. You've been hiding out, and I get that, but this… this is your shot."

I exhaled slowly, the pull of the waves tugging at something deep inside me. "It's not that simple, Jo. There's Harry. Joanna. This new life I've got… it's different. It's stable."

"But are you happy?" Jordan's question hit me like a punch to the gut, and I had to take a moment before answering. "I've seen you at your best, man. We've ridden waves together that most people only dream about. I know you've got responsibilities, but you've also got a fire in you that doesn't just go out. It's still there, isn't it?"

I glanced toward the Shack, where the sounds of the kitchen and the chatter of customers filled the air. Everything I'd worked for, everything I was building—it felt solid, real. But then there was Jordan, talking about the one thing that had always felt like home to me. Surfing wasn't just a sport; it was my identity, my way of fighting back against everything that had ever tried to pull me down.

"I won't lie," I finally said. "I do miss it. And yeah, the fire's still there. But it's complicated. The timing… it's not great."

Jordan didn't miss a beat. "When has the timing ever been

great? We've been broke, hurt, and banned from beaches, but we've always found a way. This is about more than just a competition. It's about coming back to life, Quinn. You've got something to prove—not to them, but to yourself."

His words settled over me like the pull of an incoming tide, irresistible and constant. "Alright, give me a couple of days to think about it. I need to talk to some people, figure some things out."

"Three days," Jordan agreed, his relief palpable. "Just don't make me go solo on this. We're a team, Q. We always have been."

I hung up, feeling the rush of adrenaline and uncertainty mixing inside me. The Shack was my new world, but the call of the waves, the call of who I used to be, was still there, pulling at me with a force I couldn't deny.

CHAPTER TWELVE

I went back in and finished the pots I'd left in the sink, but I was like an automaton. My mind was over two thousand miles away.

"Harry slid a plate across the counter to a waiting customer and leaned in, his voice low. "Everything okay, Kid?"

I nodded, the word 'Hawaii' sitting on my tongue like a secret promise. "Yeah, Harry, everything's just… fine." I almost bit the tip of my tongue off to keep me from spilling the news of Jordan's call. I planned to tell him eventually, of course, but I needed to turn it over a couple of times before I did. The universe had heard me, alright. Now, it was up to me to decide whether to answer its call.

The moment my shift was over, I nodded at Harry and practically sprinted for the back door.

I knew he was looking at me like I was crazy because I never left right away, but I needed a minute to myself to work through the tsunami of thoughts that Jordan's call left in its wake. Inside, the silence of the studio was a stark contrast to the chaos in my head, and I stretched out across my bed. I tried to be as objective as I could. I don't know why I wasn't jumping up and down for joy at the chance to get back out on the circuit. The Aloha Challenge could be my golden ticket, a chance to reclaim what I thought I'd lost. Instead of laying here like a sloth, why wasn't I thinking about cleaning and packing my gear? Why the heck wasn't I firing on all cylinders, amped to get back in the lineup? Winning in Hawaii again... man, that'd be the sweetest tube ride. I've done it three times, and the last time I conquered it, a monster wave that tried to chew me up and spit me out with nothing but a mouthful of sand and a broken board like the two times before. But I was ready for it that last time. I was better trained than I'd ever been. I knew what I was in for. And I was determined, hungry for that win. A comeback now would turn the lights and cameras back on and amp up the roar of the crowd.

I could almost feel the pulse of competition. And let's not forget the money. Or the sponsors. That's what I'm wired for, isn't it? The voice in my head was insistent, like the call of the ocean on a windy day. *Yeah, but what about Harry?* another little voice broke in, flashing in the front of my brain. It wasn't just about me anymore. There was Harry to think about—the old man had stuck his neck out, giving me a gig when I was about as employable as a surfer with a fear of water. Telling him I was even thinking about getting back in the game was gonna be a pretty sick conversation.

"Harry," I practiced, my voice lost to the sound of the waves. "Look, I might be hittin' up Hawaii. No biggie, right?" I snorted. No biggie. Yeah, right. It was going to be a real big biggie. I didn't know why. It's nuts how quickly the sands can shift, how someone can become your point break in a choppy sea. Harry's had my back the whole time, that's for sure, and he's done more than watch it. He's shaped me, like he's got my life under his planer, smoothing out the rough patches. This apartment, Harry's spot—it's my safe harbor after getting thrashed in the breakers of life. It's got a hold on me, like the calm at the eye of the storm. And what about the Shack? My haven, my home break. I'd be gone when the tourist tide came in high. Can I bail on that and leave my lineup short-handed? The crew's tight, and I'm a part of that set now. He'd never chain me to the Shack, but skipping out now would be like ditching your surf buddy when the swell's peaking. Not cool, not cool at all.

There's a knock at the door, a gentle rap, like the sound of a swell hitting the pier. It's gotta be Harry. I don't even have to look to know.

"You in there, Quinn?" Harry's voice is gruff but warm, like the Santa Ana winds. I chuckle despite the crossroads I'm sitting at. "Yeah, I'm good, Harry," I say, opening the door for him. His shadow fills the doorway, a silhouette against the dying light. "You ran out so quickly. I thought you maybe got some bad news."

"Nah, just an old friend from the team bringing up old memories. You wanna come in, Harry? I got a few cold ones in the fridge." He seemed to think about it for a moment, then shook his head. Maybe tomorrow night, Kid. I'm going home; put my feet up and watch the game. You sure you're gonna be okay?"

"Yeah, yeah. Sure, Harry. I'm good right now. I might go for a run on the beach."

"Maybe you ought to give that cutie pie, that surfer girl that comes in the restaurant every day, a call instead."

"No thanks. I like hanging out on Drama-Free Island," I said, thinking of Tia and Lanie.

"Alright, Kid," he said with a chuckle. "See you in the morning."

"Bright and early."

"Good night, Quinn."

"Good night, Harry."

I closed the door and blew out a long breath. See, that's what I mean, the little voice in my brain says as I head to the fridge to get myself a beer.

Harry's more than a boss—he's like the mentor I never asked for, the friend I never thought I'd find. Our bond goes beyond fish tacos and burgers and boards. Harry... the Shack... it's a makeshift family that's become my lifeboat. I've found solace in the grease and grime, the sizzle of the grill, the laughter over spilled coffee. And there's peace here, a rhythm to my days that I've come to... well, to love, honestly. The team used to call me Quinn the Quake, because they could count on me to shake things up, but maybe that's just it—I need to be grounded too, like have someplace that I don't have to blow up.

I sipped my beer and thought about my financial situation— the gnashing teeth of a topic. If Jordan and I didn't place, didn't grab some of that prize money, I'd probably be up the creek without a paddle. And not just me. The Shack wasn't exactly printing cash. Harry was banking on me being around, being that steady hand come the summer rush and helping him fix the place up during the winter lull.

I've got savings, but they're for emergencies, right? This ain't exactly an emergency. Scratching that itch to get back on the board, to feel that rush, ain't an emergency, is it?" I shook my head. That felt like leftover teenage recklessness talking. Harry and the Shack had been good to me—more than good. It's been my life raft in the stormiest sea. Bailing now felt like a betrayal. Could I do that to Harry? To myself? Was bailing on Harry worth taking a chance to stand on that podium again, feeling the weight of a medal around my neck, proving to everyone—and maybe even more to myself—that I didn't need Josh, or Sean, or Colin or anybody, to do what I do? I wasn't just any dude trying to carve up a wave; I was that dude, and I could stand tall on any podium, anywhere.

I must've fallen asleep sometime in the middle of arguing with myself. A million stars and a huge moon filled the clear night sky, and my mind was pretty much set. I was going to go to Hawaii, compete, and come home. I smiled and looked around. Yeah, this was home. At least for now, it is.

I heaved myself up off the futon and picked up the bottle I'd set on the table. I swallowed the last of the beer, and it was as warm as piss, so I must've napped at least a couple of hours. I tossed the bottle in the recycle, and went into my bedroom to pull my surfboard out of the closet and got the wax out of my duffel bag. I dug my fingers into the wax to break it up and started prepping the deck. For me, there's a calm in the routine, a focus that sharpens with each pass. Cleaning the board, applying the base coat, and then the topcoat; it's like Zen after a while. It was well into the wee hours of the morning before I was done with my boards and ready for bed.

The next day, I took Harry's advice and called up the cutie pie that comes in for lunch sometimes. It just wasn't the same cutie pie he was talking about. I sent Joanna a text asking what she was doing after work and if we could hang out. I needed a sounding board, but more than that, I needed her brand of unfiltered honesty that seemed to cut through the noise in my head. I texted her, and she agreed to meet me after she got off work. I knew her favorite place, a nice little spot where land met the sea, where thoughts could find the space to breathe and grow. She was an anchor I hadn't known I'd needed.

"Hey," I'd called out, getting out of Harry's car and taking a hesitant step in her direction.

She'd turned, and the simple kindness in her smile unwound something tight within me.

"Hey yourself," she'd greeted, and in that space between 'hello' and the rest of our conversation, I'd found the courage to bridge my past with my possible future. Joanna was perched on the edge of the pier, her feet dangling over the side like she didn't have a care in the world. I took a deep breath, tasting the salt in the air. I had always found the ocean calming, but right now, my insides were churning worse than a riptide.

"Mind if I join you?" I asked, even though I was already

dropping down beside her.

"Be my guest," she smiled, her eyes reflecting the vast expanse of dark and light blue in front of us.

I let out a sigh, not sure where to start. "So, I got a call from my friend Jordan Smith…."

Her eyebrows shot up. "The Jordan Smith? Pro surfer Jordan Smith?" She teased.

"Yeah, yeah. One and the same," I confirmed, and then spilled the whole Hawaii, Aloha Challenge, team-up proposition before I could second-guess myself.

She listened, really listened, the way the sand listens to the ocean, letting every word sink in.

"And what did you say?" she asked when I finished.

"I told him I'd think about it." I picked at a splinter on the pier, not wanting to meet her gaze.

"That sounds like a big deal, Quinn," she said softly. "Are you going for it?

"I don't know. Part of me wants to go, but the other part…I don't know.

What's holding you back?"

I shrugged. "I guess... I'm afraid of going back to that life and losing this," I gestured vaguely towards the Shack, to the pier, and to her.

Joanna turned to me, her eyes steady. "The Quinn who arrived here months ago might have lost himself in that world again. But I think the Quinn that's sitting with me right here, right now? Well, he's different. Stronger, I think."

I wanted to believe her, to believe in that version of myself. "You think so, huh?"

"I know so. Look, I've had my share of rough waters," she continued, pulling her knees to her chest. "I wanted to be a marine biologist, explore the depths, understand life in the oceans. But life... it takes you places you don't expect. My parents got sick, both at the same time, and I had to take care of them. I stayed home and got a boring job in the bank because I needed to, not because I wanted to."

Her confession hung between us like a sacred thing.

"And now?" I asked quietly.

Now? I'm okay. Dad passed, but Mom's hanging in there. But my situation is different. They depended upon me, and I was grateful to be with them and take care of them when they couldn't take care of themselves. You, however, can't let the fear of losing things or people dictate your choices. People who care about you want you to go out and try. They want you to succeed. Things? There will always be things and more things. The important things will be waiting when you get back."

Her words hit home, a direct hit to the walls I'd built around myself.

"So, you're saying I should go for it?"

She nudged me with her shoulder, a small gesture that sent ripples across my heart. "I'm just saying don't let what-ifs hold you back. Whatever you choose, it should be about moving forward, not staying still. Not hiding from yourself."

"You think that's what I'm doing?"

She shrugged, delicately lifting her shoulder to her ear. I wanted to smile—it was such a feminine thing to do—but I nodded instead, letting her know I was taking her words seriously. It was all a lot to process, but for the first time since Jordan called that, I felt like maybe, just maybe, I could find a way to ride the waves and not get pulled under.

"Thanks, Jo," I said, meaning it more than I could express.

"Anytime, surfer boy." Her smile was like a lighthouse, guiding me back to safe shores.

I still didn't know what I wanted to do, but one thing was clear—whatever decision I made about the Aloha Challenge, it wouldn't be made out of fear. And no matter where the currents took me, I knew I'd always have a piece of this place—and of Joanna—with me.

CHAPTER THIRTEEN

I was sorting through my gear when Harry called me and asked if I could come over and manage the Shack for an hour or so.

It was quiet for now, and he needed to make a grocery run for some things he'd need in the morning, and I was all too happy to do that for him. I was scrubbing down the counters when he returned, a box of fresh produce in one hand and his extra-extra-large bamboo sack in the other, filled to the brim. The Shack had been quiet the entire time, giving me just the hiss of the ocean and the occasional chatter of people out on the beach.

"Got a second, Harry?" I asked, my voice casual, hiding the weight of what I was carrying.

He grunted a yes, set the box down, and looked at me with those keen eyes that seemed to see right through you.

"I might need a couple of days off in a few weeks."

"Uhm," he grunted with a nod, and it didn't seem like he was going to help me with this at all.

Well, you remember when I got that call from an old friend," I started, watching him carefully. "It was from my teammate Jordan. He's pitching to team up for the Aloha Challenge in Hawaii.

It's only three days…." I said, my heart rate ticking up with each word. He didn't respond immediately, just gave a slow nod, the kind that told you he was processing, weighing his words.

"Three days, okay. And what did you say?" he finally asked.

"I told him I'd think about it."

"That's good. Thinking's good," Harry said, and there was a small smile there, one that didn't quite meet his eyes. I leaned back against the counter opposite him. "I don't want you to think... I mean, I haven't decided anything yet."

Harry held up a hand. "Quinn, you ever hear the saying, A man has got to have a code?"

I wasn't sure what he meant, so I just looked at him, a puzzled expression on my face…or maybe it was a painful grimace. I dunno. I was feeling both emotions at the same time.

"Well, mine's pretty simple. Honor. Courage. Commitment. I've lived by that since the Corps. It means you do what's right, even when it's hard. You face your fears, and you stick to your promises."

I shifted, uneasy under the weight of his gaze. "Sounds like the Marine Corps motto to me," I muttered.

"It is. But it ain't just for Marines. It's for life, son. If you've got a shot at something that'll make you better, you take it. That's courage. But you also remember your commitments," he continued with a pointed look at the Shack around us.

My throat felt tight. "I'm not looking to bail on you, Harry. This place... it's been more home to me than..." I trailed off, unsure how to finish.

He put a hand on my shoulder, his grip firm. "I know that. And I ain't trying to keep you tethered here, Quinn. I see the way your eyes hit the horizon every time you step on the beach. You've got the soul of a surfer, but you've also got something else. A resilience. You're not just the sum of your wins out on the waves. You've got more to offer, in or out of the water."

I swallowed and looked down at my hands, calloused and scarred from work, from life.

"Look at me," Harry's voice was gentle but insistent. I met his gaze, and there was a fierceness there. "Don't limit yourself to what you were. Think about what you could be. You've got potential, Quinn. Potential to be a hell of a lot more than just a surfer."

The words hit hard, like a rogue wave. I felt it, the shift, the quiet acknowledgment of something I hadn't let myself believe. I had been a champion on the waves, but maybe, just maybe, I could be something more on land.

I cleared my throat. "Thanks, Harry. If I go, I'll only be gone a few days. I just wanted you to know."

The silence spun out for a couple of minutes before he spoke again.

"You know," he began, a faraway look in his eyes. "I didn't build this place as my end game." I turned to look at him, surprised by the admission.

"No?" I asked, genuinely curious.

He shook his head, a distant look in his eyes. "No, it was a stepping-stone. A place to land while I figured things out. Life has a funny way of... changing the plans you set out for yourself."

CHAPTER
FOURTEEN

I could feel the weight of Harry's words, heavy with unspoken stories.

"Is that what you think the Shack is for me?" The question came out softer than I intended.

Harry's gaze snapped back to the present, locking onto mine. "It could be. Or it could be more, depends on what you need, what you want from it."

I thought about that, about what the Shack had become for me —a refuge, a place to rebuild. But was it just a stop or a layover in my journey? It didn't feel like it. It felt solid, more like a home than anywhere I ever stayed, including my folks' place. That had never felt like home.

"You've got a whole world beyond these walls, Quinn," Harry said, gesturing to the Shack. "This place, it's important, sure. But it ain't the whole sky. Don't get me wrong, you're damn good for the Shack, but I won't let it be the anchor that keeps you from sailing."

My chest tightened at his words. Harry, this gruff ex-Marine, saw beyond the horizon for me, even when I couldn't.

"And if the Shack is just a small part of your journey, that's okay. You've brought life to it and given me a bit of hope, too. But don't you dare think this is all you're capable of."

I felt a shift inside, like a sail catching a new wind. Harry was giving me an out, but more than that, he was giving me an 'in' to something bigger within myself.

"Harry, I—"

He held up a hand. "You don't gotta say anything now. Just promise me you'll think bigger than the waves and this old place. You're not made to stay docked."

The commitment in his tone was like a challenge, one that stirred something deep within me. Harry had given me a haven, but he was also pushing me to see that I could be more than just a part of the scenery here.

I nodded, the possibilities churning like the tide. "I promise, Harry."

He clapped me on the back. "That's all I'm asking. You think on your future, then you follow your gut. And whatever you decide, I'll be right here, backing you up."

The emotion was there, in the catch of his voice, in the steadfast presence he offered. It wasn't a bleeding heart; it was solid, real. It was Harry. We sat there for a while, two men staring out at the sea, both lost in thoughts of what was and what could be. Harry had opened a door, and now it was up to me to decide whether to step through it.

A couple of days later, I was dragging my board up past the tide line, a prickly mix of salt and sand clinging to my skin, and

I caught a glimpse of something unexpected. Harry was standing off to the side, his eyes fixed on the horizon—or were they on me? I couldn't help the tightness that grabbed my chest. It wasn't just a passing glance. It was a kind of intense, all-in stare that you'd crave from someone who mattered—a coach, a mentor... a father. Not that I'd know too much about that last one. For years, I'd ridden waves, chasing that perfect high, the cheering crowds a blurry backdrop. But my dad? He never showed. No proud cheers, no waiting glances. Just me and an indifferent ocean as a constant spectator. Until Harry.

Seeing him there, I was suddenly fourteen again—raw and hungry for that nod of approval. I paused, a lump forming in my throat, and for a heartbeat, the rest of the world faded out. It was just Harry and the unspoken acknowledgment that he was here for me. Lifting my hand, I pushed past the lump, past the years of indifference, and sent a thumbs-up his way. I didn't do it for the acknowledgment or because it was expected. I did it because, for the first time in a long while, I felt seen.

He didn't need to shout, clap, or make a scene. His silent vigil spoke volumes, and as he nodded, as was his habit, and turned back towards the Shack, his presence locked in something vital. And for a guy whose own father never gave a damn, it meant more than any trophy ever could.

Later, when the night had tucked the beach away, I sat with Harry in the tiny courtyard between the Shack and the garage we used mainly for storage with my apartment on top. a couple of cold brews between us. We'd just polished off a feast that Harry had whipped up just for us—massive scallops, crispy shrimp, killer calamari, and crab, that had us feeling like a couple of beached whales, super satisfied but also super chill. A couple of cracked, chilled brews sat on the table in front of us. Mine had been barely touched. The courtyard was quiet, but I'd turned on the fairy lights hanging above it. Harry had snorted when he came out with the food but hadn't said anything. I picked up my bottle and took a long swallow, then fixing my gaze on one of the lights, I finally I said, "I'm going to Hawaii, Harry."

He didn't speak immediately, but when he did, his voice was gruff with pride.

"I knew you were, Quinn. You've got the look of a man who'd decided to take on the world."

I could only nod, feeling that, yeah, maybe I was taking on the world or at least my fears. It was as much a battle as any wave I'd ever faced. I suppose that was all that needed saying as we sat there companionably until the first stars winked into life above us, and the ocean continued its rhythmic push and pull. Harry put his feet up in another of the chairs around the table and finished off another beer. I slouched down in my seat, my head resting on the chair back, and nursed mine, feeling utterly content.

The morning air was already buzzing with that electric charge that came right before dawn. I had my alarm set, but who was I kidding? I hadn't slept a wink. My mind was a whirlpool, circling the same thought—I was going back to Hawaii, back to competing. I was out the door while the world was still painted in shades of grey, the morning sun still lurking below the eastern horizon.

The only sound was the distant murmur of the ocean and the soft thud of my running shoes hitting the sand. My breath came out in steady puffs, visible in the cool morning air, a testament to the work I was already putting in.

This was the first day of my new regime—before work, after work, any damn moment I could steal. I felt that old familiar burn in my lungs, the ache in my muscles, but it was good, it was right. It was the pain of progress, of building towards something that mattered.

As I ran, I replayed competitions in my mind. The buzz of the crowd, the salt spray kicking up from the break, the announcer calling out names. I could feel it, almost hear and taste it. It was a heady mix of nerves and excitement, but beneath it all was this steady current of purpose. I was doing this for me, not for sponsors, not for glory, not to prove something to Jordan.

I put in four miles and when I got back to the beach in front of the Shack, the first fingers of sunlight were stretching across the sky, painting everything in gold and pink. The ocean was a sheet of glass, waiting for the day to stir it up. I ditched my shoes and set out at a sprint, feeling that connection to the earth, raw and immediate. I dove into the waves, the shock of the cold a welcome slap, and I came up for air and started paddling out, every stroke a statement. This was my turf, my battleground, and with every passing second, I felt more alive than I had in months. I also felt good—focused and strong, like my old self. With the water all around me and dawn breaking like a promise, I set out like a dolphin back to shore, swimming with more power than I'd mustered in a long time.

By mid-afternoon, the Shack was in its usual swing—tourists like seagulls, locals like the steady rocks they perch on. But today, as I flipped fries, dressed burgers and fish sandwiches, and blended fruit drinks, there was a new rhythm to my movements, a new hum under my breath. My decision was made. I was going, and the air around me seemed to crackle with it, charged with the energy of my quiet resolve. Harry noticed, of course. He always does, and his knowing gaze caught mine in the ebb of customer flow, a silent nod passing between us. He didn't say anything, but his eyes did the talking: "You're doing the right thing, Kid."

After my shift, I ran up the stairs to my apartment and changed clothes. The cool whisper of the ocean breeze called me back to the waves but today I had another kind of training to attend to. I set out, taking the crooked, quiet streets past old and dilapidated commercial buildings covered in bright graffiti to the quiet backstreet gym where old fight posters peeled on the walls, and the scent of determination was stronger than the musty sweat. It was perfect for what I needed. I paid for a month in advance, with cash, and the owner—a burly guy with a nose that told stories of its own—raised an eyebrow. "Preparing for something big?"

"You could say that," I replied, anxious to get started.

The weights didn't care about my surfing career, my failures, or my fears. They were indifferent, solid, and real. They were the gravity I needed to pull myself away from the endless float, the tether to a goal that was larger than the swell.

I started with the bench press, the clink of metal on metal, a steady metronome to my thoughts. Each rep was a stroke, each set a wave, every drop of sweat a mile traveled toward Hawaii. With every lift, I pushed against my past, my limitations, my self-doubt.

And then, onto the pull-ups, my arms and back engaging in a silent war against my own weight. It was grueling, but it was a conversation, a debate between my body and spirit.

"Can we do this?"

"We must."

"Will we succeed?"

"We'll give it our all."

~

The evening had settled like a soft blanket over the beach by the time I got back from the gym. The usual tension that lived between my shoulder blades, coiled like a spring, had eased. I felt solid and grounded, like I'd laid the first stone on a path that was meant for me.

I stood outside, just a silhouette against the fading light, my eyes on the small studio that had become my sanctuary. It wasn't much—three rooms and a window that looked out over the world I knew. But it was mine. And for a long while, it was enough. My gaze drifted beyond that window, past the immediate horizon, to the outlines of dreams I had dared not chase. In the stillness, my mind buzzed. I could almost hear the waves of Hawaii and feel the challenges they presented. The Aloha Challenge was no longer a distant idea; it was a calling. It whispered of risk, of reward, and of the rush that comes from knowing you've set your sights on something that truly tests you. I needed to see the ocean, needed to feel its pull. With a deep breath, I ran upstairs, grabbed my board and headed back down to the shore, my bare feet padding against the cool sand. There was no one else around, just me, the moon, the stars, and the sea.

The water was dark, but it didn't scare me. It was an old friend, an old adversary. I waded in, the familiar chill wrapping around my ankles, then my waist. When I paddled out, each stroke was a promise. I wasn't leaving the Shack, wasn't leaving my life. I was taking a part of it with me, a part that would grow with every mile I put between myself and this beach, and I would be back. I'd be back in a couple of days, and I'd come back after every competition.

The ocean held me like it knew. It knew I was coming to make peace with it in a place where it was strongest. As I lay on my board, the swell gentle beneath me, I let myself feel it all—the fear, the excitement, the uncertainty. "Hawaii," I whispered to the stars, a vow between me and the universe. And I could swear, in the quiet that followed, the waves whispered back, "We'll be waiting." In that moment, I knew I was ready. I wasn't just going to Hawaii to compete. I was going to show myself I could do it on my own.

The paddle back to shore was slow and meditative. Each stroke was a step toward a future I was ready to embrace. And when I reached the sand, I stood and looked back at the sea, a sentinel guarding the night.

"Aloha," I said with a grin, feeling the weight of my board under my arm, the salt on my skin, the determination in my bones. I'd be damned if I wouldn't give it 110 percent.

CHAPTER FIFTEEN

December twentieth kind of snuck up on me, and as I got dressed for work, I realized that today was my birthday.

In all of my twenty-three years, everything felt different somehow. In my family, birthdays were always treated as if they were just another day. Mom and I would always acknowledge that I was another year older, but never in front of my brother or my dad. It was our quiet tradition, just between the two of us, and though there were never any presents or fanfare, I held on to those special moments when Mom would whisper happy birthday to me. I used to marvel at how most people treated their birthdays as if they ranked right up there with Christmas or New Year's Eve. But, today I felt just a little bit special and that I should celebrate.

This morning, as a little treat to myself, I'd gone out right at dawn with my board and stayed on the water a little longer, surfing the waves that kept rolling in like pile drivers. I felt at home out there, the rhythm of the ocean washing over me, giving me a sense of peace I rarely found anywhere else. Afterward, I paddled back to shore, feeling the exhilaration of a perfect session, like the ocean had given me a gift only I could unwrap.

When I got back to my apartment over the garage, I showered and changed, getting ready for another day at the Shack. As I pulled on my clothes, my phone buzzed on the bathroom counter. I glanced down, expecting another random notification, but when I saw Jordan's name flashing on the screen, I picked it up, a smile tugging at my lips.

"Happy birthday, old man!" Jordan's voice boomed through the phone, filled with that familiar energy that always lifted my spirits.

"Thanks, Jo," I said, laughing. "How did you remember?"

"Are you kidding? We're family, man. I had it on my calendar. Plus, you're only a year behind me. Gotta remind you every chance I get."

His call was the first, but it wasn't the last. Gray called next, then Lloyd, each of them reaching out separately to wish me a happy birthday. It was loud and chaotic, each conversation a little piece of home, and for a moment, it felt like old times.

Each call was like a jolt of the past—Lloyd's greetings, Gray's gruff but genuine wishes, Maldonado's jokes, and Jordan's relentless cheer. I'd even received texts from Josh, Sean, Marc, Vince, and Jeff. They didn't have to do it, but they did, and it meant more than I could say. Those small gestures, sending me their heartfelt wishes, made me feel connected in a way I hadn't felt even when we were all together.

When I arrived for work, Harry told me traffic in the Shack had been slow all morning, more than usual, and as I looked around, the place seemed too quiet. It was already past noon, and we'd usually be slammed by now. Harry said only a few people had trickled in for carry-out. The dining room was empty, still gleaming after the scrubbing I'd given it the night before, unable to tempt even those few souls who'd stopped through for their carryout to take a seat and enjoy their food. I was not used to having time like this on my hands. Harry seemed to be in his own little world, answering me when I asked a question, but he didn't seem to have any anecdotes or morality stories to share. I should've been glad, but the Shack felt empty, and not even the Christmas music piped in as background cheered me up. I decided to go to the back, straighten up in the kitchen and take care of the few pots Harry had used. It was a little soon to take inventory, but I had the time, so that was next on my list. I was in the zone when Harry called me.

"Hey Quinn, can you lend a hand with this?" He called from the dining room, and I thought something was amiss.

"Sure, Harry," I said, pulling off my apron. "What's up?"

As I rounded the corner, the lights flicked on, and a chorus of "Surprise!" filled the room. My heart skipped a beat. The entire place was full, people holding balloons and shining flashlights from their phones. Some were even taking pictures. Harry stood at the front, a wide grin on his weather-beaten face, holding a cake that was awkwardly lopsided but earnestly decorated.

"Happy Birthday, Kid. Didn't think we'd forget, did you?"

I was speechless, my eyes darting around the room. Joanna was there, her smile as warm as the summer sun, and a lot of regulars, some of whom I'd only known by their lunch orders. They were all grinning back at me. Harry started singing Happy Birthday in his scratchy baritone, and the crowd joined in. All I could do was laugh and enjoy the attention.

"Come on, make a wish!" Harry nudged, lighting two candles that gave away my age, a two and a three, and the room fell into an expectant hush. I leaned forward, the flickering candles casting playful shadows on the faces around me—faces that had become a part of my new life. I closed my eyes for a moment, feeling a wave of gratitude. The wish? That was a secret, but the warmth in the room was all the confirmation I needed that it was already coming true. I blew out the candles to a round of applause.

Harry, with his usual flair, sliced the cake into generous portions while Joanna passed around drinks. The laughter and chatter filled the Shack—so much laughter and chatter that it filled me with so much happiness I felt like I had helium in my chest. As I took a bite of the hunk of chocolate marble cake that he'd handed me, Mr. Peterson came over and gave me a high-five.

"You're one of us now, Quinn. This place wouldn't be the same without you." That was probably the most I'd ever heard him say in a single breath, and I beamed and nodded like a bobblehead. Done passing out drinks, Joanna came over and sat next to me to eat her more modest slice of care.

"Happy birthday, Quinn."

"Thanks, Jo. You guys really got me. I was gonna suggest to Harry to close up shop early, but then he popped this on me. You guys totally surprised me."

"I'm glad. Harry was so excited to do something special for

you."

"Heck, this tops it. I can't remember the last time I had a birthday party."

"Well, enjoy. I've got to get back to work. I just wanted to be here to help surprise you. Maybe we can hang out later?"

"Yeah, I mean, sure. I'd like that. Want me to pick you up from work?"

"Nah, I'll drive over," she said. My brows shot up, and I looked at her surprised. I didn't know she had wheels, but why wouldn't she? "I haven't seen your apartment yet." She gave me a big grin and a wave goodbye.

I looked around, taking in the rest of my guests—the makeshift family I hadn't known I needed. Harry, Pete and the rest of the gang realized that here, amid the laughter and camaraderie, I found a slice of home. This wasn't just a birthday celebration; it was a reminder of the unexpected ties that bind us, the joy found in simple moments, and the beauty of a life that's shared, even in the smallest of seaside shacks.

Joanna invited me to go Christmas shopping with her this afternoon, and though I rarely shopped in the stores, I was geeked to be with her. She said she was pretty much done with her list and only needed a few more things, but I hadn't even started. I didn't have too many people to shop for this year. I could pick something up for Harry and Joanna, and I wanted to send my mother some money. She preferred cash, so I'd reload her debit card while we were out.

I wondered how she was doing and if my father and brother

were okay. Chris was older than me and a carbon copy of our father. We all had our issues, though I doubt any of us were diagnosed. Sometimes, my depression might get out of hand, but I'm always able to bounce back. Dad and Chris, however, needed real help. I looked it up once, and something called antisocial personality disorder fit Dad to a tee.

Shoving thoughts of my family away, I got dressed, grabbed my phone and wallet, and hurried downstairs. I never went shopping with a chick before. I was always too busy doing my thing, or I just didn't want to. I've bought gifts for them before, like little pieces of jewelry or trinkets they liked, but I've never walked around the stores with one before. I don't know why going with Joanna would seem fun, but it did, and I'd probably know a lot more about her after spending the afternoon with her. Unfortunately, I laughed to myself, she might know a lot more about me. But I wouldn't want it any other way.

It was chilly enough for us to wear lightweight jackets, even in full sun. The shopping concourse was bustling with people in the Christmas spirit. Palm trees were adorned with twinkling lights, and there were lots of Santas with happy smiles, dressed in Hawaiian shirts, some sipping tropical drinks and riding surfboards. In nearly all of the stores, employees wore Santa and Elf caps and bubbly smiles. We wandered in and out of the open-air market, a vibrant tapestry of local crafts and seasonal treats, and I hadn't seen anything that caught my eye.

"So, what are you getting, Harry?" Joanna asked, her sunglasses perched atop her head as we browsed a stall with handcrafted woodwork.

"I don't know. I don't know if I should get him something for *him*, or for the Shack. I don't know what he needs or likes," I mused, examining a set of intricately carved drink coasters. "Do you like these?

"Uhm, no. Not as a gift. We'll find something else. I got you something, too," Joanna teased with a playful nudge.

"Yeah? What?"

"You'll just have to wait for Christmas to see. You don't have to get me anything. When I saw your gift, I got it. It reminded me of you." I looked at her, seeing her beautiful brown eyes and heart-shaped face, and I wanted to take her in my arms and kiss her right then and there. She had a way of moving me. I couldn't begin to imagine what she could have found that reminded her of me. I took her hand and led us away from the vendor's table. We continued our stroll, and I discreetly tried to note anything that sparked an idea for Joanna's gift. I'd seen a delicate necklace with a sea glass pendant in a small jewelry stall we'd passed earlier that I liked. Glancing at her slender throat, I could easily imagine it resting above her cleavage. It was elegant, just like her. I'd find a way to go back and get it before we left.

After helping her pick out a few more gifts for friends and family, I led us on a detour to a couple of the surf shops.

"You can't be done with your Christmas shopping without having checked out the surf gear," I protested and led her inside. I admit I found looking at the gear a lot more interesting than she did. I made a note of the various manufacturers and brands, debated the merits of various board designs, and laughed over quirky t-shirts. I bought a few things, mostly quirky souvenirs for Joanna and some triple-X tee shirts for Harry. They weren't meant to be Christmas gifts; it just felt like I was sharing a piece of my world with them, and Joanna's happy laughter was the best gift I could ask for.

When we got hungry, we settled at a picnic table in the outdoor food court and lingered over grilled paninis and iced coffees in the waning warmth of the late afternoon sun. The sound of waves provided a soothing backdrop, a reminder of the ever-present ocean steps away.

"Thank you for hanging out with me today, Quinn. I know guys hate shopping with girls, but I had fun," Joanna said, her hand sliding across the table to find mine. I clasped her hand and gave it a squeeze.

"I had fun too, believe it or not," I replied. Realizing that I had. It was one of the most relaxing, carefree days I'd had in months. "Do you mind sitting here with our stuff? Do you need anything?" I asked, getting up. She shook her head, and I told her, "I'll be right back." I remembered where the little jewelry stall was and headed in that direction.

Finding it, I showed the woman behind the table the necklace I wanted and a pair of tiny sea glass earrings that matched it. I pulled out my platinum card from my wallet and swiped it. The lady gift-wrapped it for me in silvery green paper with a matching bow and put it in a pretty little shopping bag. I didn't want Joanna to see it, so I slipped the box into the inside pocket of my jacket and handed the bag back to the lady.

We stayed a little longer, and I picked up a few more things for Harry that I knew he wouldn't necessarily buy for himself, including a high-quality chef's knife set and an ergonomic floor mat the store owner swore would provide comfort and reduce strain on Harry's knees that came from standing all day.

"So, what are you thinking of getting your family?" Joanna asked as we headed back to her car. We filled the trunk with her stuff and put my bags on the back seat. She climbed behind the wheel, and I got in, riding shotgun. I smiled slightly as I thought about all the things I would have liked to do for Mom. She might have liked the gold earrings I saw in the jewelry shop or a warm shawl, but I knew she wouldn't wear them because Dad would cause an uproar when he saw them.

"Mom's very practical. She appreciates having a little money to buy the extras she wants and needs."

Joanna nodded understandingly. "That's great. It's always nice to shop for what you want."

"Are you going to see your family for the holidays?"

"Nah," I said, thinking to myself that if there was a worse time to visit, the holidays topped the list. Joanna didn't say anything, and I didn't offer an explanation.

We drove back to the Shack, and she followed me upstairs. Since seeing my apartment for the first time on my birthday, she'd come over every evening after work and hung out with me on her days off. I kept the place spotlessly clean and fresh, and we usually grabbed something to eat at the Shack. Afterward, we'd cuddle up and watch a movie or something on the massive TV I'd gifted myself.

CHAPTER SIXTEEN

After considerable thought, I decided I would meet Jordan in Hawaii for the Aloha Challenge.

But because it was scheduled to start on the twenty-sixth, that meant that I wouldn't get to spend Christmas Day with Harry or Joanna. And I only had two days to get all my stuff together and book a last-minute flight. I found one leaving out early Christmas morning and scrambled around, trying to decide what to take and what to leave. I also needed to pack my other gear— wetsuits, goggles, wax, and things like that. Every few minutes I thought of something I would need and had to run back up to the apartment and toss it on my bed. I'd never been so scatter-brained before or so nervous.

When I finally came back down to work after the fourth or fifth time, Harry just shooed me away, sending me back upstairs to get myself together. But instead of returning to the apartment and doing the right thing, I went to the gym instead. It was mostly empty, just a few other souls in their own worlds of exertion, and I liked it that way. This was my last session here, and the solitude greeted me as I walked in. I needed to work off all the electrifying tension that was zinging in my bloodstream, and I just hoped I wouldn't wreck the equipment.

As I wrapped up with the leg presses, pushing against the weight as I'd push against the force of the ocean, I felt a clarity I hadn't known in a long time. The gym was my crucible, the weights my foes, and as I walked out, muscles singing and spirit lifted, the streetlights blinked on like a standing ovation. Returning to the apartment, I was greeted with what looked like a tsunami had blasted through. I fell onto the edge of my bed, groaning like an old man settling into his favorite chair. I was too tired and too sore to feel like doing it right now. Besides, I was crap at packing. I could cram a van for a surf trip with my eyes shut, but a suitcase or my duffel bag? That was a different story. Every fold of a shirt, every coil of a leash, felt heavy with intent. My boards were waxed and raring to go, propped up against the wall, watching me like a faithful hound. The rest of my gear was scattered across the room, a mess of neoprene, sunscreen, and ambition. I got up and took a deep breath, full of resolve. My feet shuffled across the carpet, began picking up clothes and sorting them into piles. I snagged my favorite board shorts, the ones that had seen more saltwater than a sea turtle, and I laid them out. They'd ride the Hawaiian waves with me. A good luck charm? Maybe. Or maybe just a scrap of the familiar when everything else was spinning into the new and unknown.

After a while, I had a few small loads and put half of them into the small stacked washer at the end of the galley kitchen. While they washed and dried, I packed my duffel with more care. All my gear went inside, and the last thing I wanted was to leave something behind or have it ripped or ruined by the time I got to Hawaii. I carefully put my boards in their travel carrier and zipped them in snugly. Propping everything by the door, the apartment was looking better.

There's a weird dance you do when you're on the cusp of something huge—part jitterbug, part tightrope—and it was a huge kick. I was caught up in the anticipation, the wild pulse of it all. Harry's words echoed in my skull as I polished every square inch of each room, "Don't get caught in the undertow, Kid." I smiled. I knew what he meant more than waves, and we both knew it. But hell, what's life without a bit of a tumble in the surf?

I glanced over at the tiny window that looked out towards the ocean, sunlight slicing through the pane like a laser. Yeah, I'd be leaving this nook of safety, this little slice of paradise I'd stitched together from scraps of loss and tattered ideas to chase a dream, but I wasn't the same dude who washed up here months ago. I had a fire burning in my chest now, stoked by a sergeant with a heart of gold and a scrappy girl with a laugh that could light up the coast.

Putting the stick vac away, I felt a chapter closing. Not the book, not the story, but a chapter. And that was cool. That's how it's supposed to go. You ride one wave to the shore, and then you paddle back out for the next one. The Aloha Challenge wasn't just a competition. It was the next wave, and I was damn glad I'd decided to take it.

CHAPTER SEVENTEEN

I was ready when a knock cracked against the door.

Though it was still dark outside, the sun hadn't yet made its appearance for the day. I knew it was Harry. I grinned as I opened the door.

"Hey, Kid," he said, his voice a gravel road that had seen plenty of travel.

"Hey, Harry." I managed a smile, one that carried all the miles of the journey ahead.

He stepped in, taking a last look around the room that had been mine. "You got everything?"

"Yeah, all packed up." I patted the bag. "Just the board, my duffel, and me."

Harry nodded, the lines in his face deepening with pride, or maybe something else. "You're ready for this."

It wasn't a question. It was a recognition of the work I'd put in, of the hours spent in the water and the gym, of the mental battles fought and won.

"I am," I said, the words as much an affirmation for myself as they were a response to him.

He clapped a hand on my shoulder, his grip firm. "Remember, whatever happens out there, you're riding those waves for you. Not for anyone else. You hear?"

I heard. And more than that, I understood.

We stepped outside, and the night air was cool, a contrast to the warmth I felt at the center of my chest. We didn't speak as we walked to the car, but we didn't need to. The silence was comfortable, filled with unsaid things that didn't need voicing.

I loaded my bag into the trunk and turned to look at the Shack. This wasn't goodbye, no matter what.

As Harry started the engine, I rolled down the window and let the breeze play through my fingers. We drove toward the airport, the Shack shrinking behind us, but it wasn't shrinking inside me. It was coming with me in every lesson learned, every burger flipped, every quiet moment shared. The Shack was part of my foundation, and no matter how high I'd build from here, it would always be part of the structure that held me steady.

"Catch some waves for me, huh?" Harry's voice broke the silence as the airport came into view.

I smiled broadly, feeling the surge of my heart, the wave already building beneath me. "Count on it, Harry. I'll catch enough for us both."

And with that promise hanging in the air, I climbed out of the passenger door and went around to the truck to start unloading it. I was only going to be gone five days, but I had so much stuff to take with me. Harry helped me hoist everything onto my back and shoulders and gave me a fatherly hug and a couple of firm slaps across my chest. It was about as emotional as I'd ever seen him, and it filled my heart. With eyes burning from tears I refused to shed, I gave him one last nod and headed inside the airport to my assigned gate.

CHAPTER EIGHTEEN

Stepping off the plane, the Hawaiian air hit me like a warm wave—none of that recycled plane funk.

I couldn't tell you if the flight was bumpy or smooth because I was riding a different kind of air up there, one made of nerve and stoke. The anticipation in my chest made it hard to focus on the flight's turbulence or smoothness. I didn't need the captain to announce our arrival; I knew exactly where we were, pulsing to the rhythm of distant ukuleles and crashing shores.

Juggling my bags and boards, I wove through the crowd skillfully, spotting Jordan in the sea of faces. He hadn't changed much—still had that shark's grin that said he was ready to take a bite out of life. Jordan slapped my palm. No words were needed when you've got a shared history like we had. I loaded my gear in the back of the hotel shuttle, and we drove along the scenic Kamehameha highway. The main hotel where most of the surfers were staying was nice, considering it was all floral prints and aloha smiles. We might have charmed the lady at the front desk, or maybe everyone in Hawaii just runs on island time and good vibes. Our rooms had a view of the ocean that was picture perfect —you know, swaying palms and a sunset glow. The room itself was a comforting oasis amid the unknowns of competition. But the real deal was at the competition desk, where a quick check-in had our names inked into the roster. No turning back now.

We all knew the dance—shake hands, slap a few backs, size up the competition like a couple of wildcards had been thrown into the mix. The camaraderie among the surfers was palpable, a silent recognition of the shared pursuit of mastery over the waves. Then, just like that, it was done. The pieces were in place: the board, the buddy, the beach. It was all a whirlwind that tasted of salt and possibility, but it was the good kind of chaos—the kind you ride, not the kind that rides you.

After a brief break to shower and change into shorts and a Hawaiian shirt, Jordan and I split up before dinner. I wanted to get a feel for where we'd be competing in the morning. The beach was electric, charged with the collective energy of anticipation and raw nerve. Tents and banners flapped in the coastal breeze like the flags of an invading army, each one staking claim to a piece of the beach. The entire beach was a canvas of anticipation. Each surfer was an artist preparing to paint their masterpiece on the waves. I walked out to the waterline and stood on the sands of destiny—or the surfer's Mecca where legends are made and wiped out with the same breathless fervor—or whatever poetic crap you wanna call it. But to me, I was on the proving ground, the place where I was going to write the story of the comeback kid, not in a novel, but on these waves. Already,

I could feel the energy of the ocean seeping into my spirit, infusing it with the spirit of every surfer who had ever dared to conquer these waters. I was pumped.

Turning away, I looked for a quiet spot away from the hubbub. Surfers, like knights before a joust, were spread out across the sand, prepping their gear, waxing their boards, and swapping tales of waves conquered and storms braved. There was a fraternity here, but also the unspoken knowledge that tomorrow, out on the water, it would be every surfer for themselves. The camaraderie on the shore was soon to be replaced by the fierce competition in the waves.

I found a spot where the sound of the ocean could speak to me without interruption. It was time to turn inward, to draw on the months of preparation, the early mornings and late nights at the Shack, every word of encouragement Harry had ever tossed my way like a lifeline. In my mind, I ran through tomorrow's routine—wake up, stretch, have a light breakfast, and then go to the beach to claim my spot in the lineup. Visualization was key; I had to see myself on the waves, feel the ebb and flow, the push and pull of the tide, the rush of the ride.

That evening, all of the competitors ate dinner at the hotel, which was like an all-inclusive resort. We had been given dinner tickets, which we had to surrender as we entered the Luau the hotel was hosting for us. We were ushered into an enchanting outdoor setting, surrounded by swaying palm trees and the gentle rustle of tropical foliage. It was a paradise within paradise, a hidden gem where nature's beauty played a central role. Upon our arrival, we were met with warm smiles and the fragrant embrace of fresh flower leis. The delicate petals adorning our necks symbolized the genuine hospitality of the Hawaiian people.

There was a bar off to the side and I grabbed a cold beer, taking it with me into the luau. This was not my first luau, but it was undoubtedly the most sumptuous feast I'd ever seen. The buffet overflowed with traditional Hawaiian dishes, each a culinary masterpiece. My taste buds danced as I savored the smoky tenderness of Kalua Pig, the earthy richness of Laulau, and the unique texture of Poi. The flavors transported me to a realm of pure delight.

At full dark, the gentle strumming of ukuleles filled the air. Live musicians serenaded us with melodies that whispered of Hawaiian legends and ocean breezes. The hauntingly beautiful hula dances brought stories to life through graceful movements and colorful costumes. It was as if the very essence of Hawaii was dancing before our eyes. Then, the night came alive with the mesmerizing spectacle of the fire dancers. They moved with precision and grace, their torches casting a mesmerizing glow against the darkening sky. The flames seemed to mimic the fiery spirit of the islands. I found myself drawn into the festivities, swaying to the music and attempting to mimic the fluid motions of the hula dancers. Laughter and camaraderie filled the air as we all became part of this vibrant celebration.

It was a lot of fun, but it also made me feel something akin to homesickness. Surrounded by the sights, sounds, and flavors of Hawaii, I missed my friends. Not Jordan or the other knuckleheads trying to crack coconuts like they'd been shown by one of the native performers. The friends of my heart, my new, true family. Harry and Joanna. I wished they were with me, enjoying this feast for the senses and celebrating the spirit of aloha. Sitting in the midst of two hundred or more people, I missed their company.

CHAPTER NINETEEN

The next morning, the first fingers of dawn hadn't yet pried open the night when I hit the sand, board under my arm, the world around me just a whisper.

The beach was different in the early morning light like it was holding its breath, waiting for the day to ignite. I had my rituals, things I'd done before every competition since I was a kid. A run along the water's edge, the cold foam chasing my steps, a set of stretches that made my muscles sing, and a moment with my eyes closed, just listening to the rhythm of the sea. It was my way of syncing up with the ocean, of saying, 'I'm here, let's do this.'

The air was thick with the scent of salt and wax, and I could feel the pulse of the beach start to quicken, the arrival of spectators like the incoming tide. There was an energy building, the same kind that buzzed through your veins before a big set rolled in. The anticipation was palpable, a shared feeling among all the surfers, a mixture of excitement and nerves that made the challenge ahead even more exhilarating.

I caught sight of a few familiar faces, the kind that brought back a flood of memories—bright days and wipe-outs, victories and losses. They nodded at me, a couple of 'good lucks' thrown around, but we all knew luck was just a small part of it. The unspoken bond of the surfing community ran deep, and while we were all competitors in the water, we were also comrades in the pursuit of riding the perfect wave.

I was half in my head, half in the moment. Visions of past glories flickered behind my lids, each one a stepping-stone that had led to now. But this wasn't about the past. This was about the wave in front of me, the here and now. The memories of past victories and defeats served as a reminder of the journey that had brought me to this point, but the focus was squarely on the challenge ahead.

As I made my way to the water's edge, the sun broke free, setting the ocean ablaze with morning light. The rising sun painted the sky and water with a golden hue, and as I looked out at the rising swell, I could feel it all coming together—the kid who lived for the rush, the guy who'd lost his way, and the man who'd found something like peace. They were all here with me, ready to face whatever this Challenge had in store.

By eight o'clock, the beach was a hive of activity, a sea of competitors and fans buzzing with excitement. The announcer's voice boomed over the loudspeaker, declaring the start of the heats and I walked towards the shoreline, Jordan at my side. We weren't in the first set, but we wanted a good look at our competition. I shook my arms and legs out, trying to shake off some of the energy that had built up all morning. There's something about pre-competition jitters that gets your blood pumping harder than any double espresso ever could, and I could feel the buzz, electric and alive, zinging through my veins.

Big day, Q," Jordan said, clapping me on the back, his eyes lit with the same fire I felt burning inside me.

"Yeah, biggest yet," I replied, my voice steady, even if my insides were doing acrobatics.

We scoped out the competition. There were a few faces I knew from the circuit, but mostly everyone else was a new kid on the block, hungry for a piece of glory. They all had that look in their eyes, the one that said they were ready to own the ocean. I felt like an old man next to them, though I was only twenty-three. I had so much more experience than they had.

When it was our set, the six of us, Jordan, me, and the two other crews formed a line. I paddled out, my arms cutting through the water, every stroke shaking off a layer of doubt. The ocean welcomed me like an old friend, and I paddled out to the line with purpose, feeling the power of the sea beneath me. I was first up, and when a strong wave approached, a towering crest of water, challenging yet inviting, I got in front of it, positioning myself and feeling the wave lift me. I stood tall on my board, my body and mind in harmony with the surf. The wave wasn't a barrel, but it offered its own kind of dance, and I carved up its face, tracing arcs of spray with each turn. My movements felt fluid, my skill taking over, and I connected with the motion of the wave.

The crowd roared from the shore, their cheers blending with the roar of the waves, and my heart raced with each turn, my focus absolute. I executed a series of rapid snaps and cutbacks, displaying my control and agility for the judges. As the wave began to lose its energy, I made a final, graceful cut before hopping off the back of the wave. Throwing a triumphant fist in the air, I felt exhilarated. The announcer's voice boomed, though I was too excited to make out the words, but I knew I couldn't have given a better performance.

Jordan was next, matching my fervor with his style. His surfing was a blend of power and grace, each move a display of his sheer will to win. He looked like he was performing a high-speed ballet on water, every step and maneuver perfectly executed. I was not above bragging, but the bar had been raised, and I was sure everyone knew it.

Back on the shore, we shared a look of triumph, knowing we'd delivered something special. The judges' scores came in at more than enough to advance us to the next round. Back on the sand, while waiting for our next heat, some of our competitors passed by, some stopping to exchange fist bumps and small talk. They were a mix of old faces and new—some remembered me, others knew only the name and the story that came with it.

There were about thirty minutes between heats, so Jordan and I huddled down by our boards, analyzing the ever-changing waves. As we strategized, a familiar face from back in the day came over and gave me a fist bump. Junior Nash and I had surfed in events like this for a couple of years before Colin tagged me to join Josh's team. I was happy to see him.

"Q? Man, how are you doing? I'm surprised to see you out

here. I heard about Josh and Colin. Dude, that was hard to swallow."

"Yeah, it was. Junior, this is my teammate Jordan. Jordan, Junior. We surfed together back in the day. So, how have you been?"

"Good. Haven't quite made it to your level, but it's been good. Trying to pick up some new sponsors. Left my team after a… disagreement, I guess you could call it."

"You doing the circuit on your own?"

"For now. Hoping a few sponsors will bite. How about you? You're off the big circuits?"

I shrugged, offering a noncommittal smile. "Just taking it one wave at a time. Trying to keep our edge, you know?"

"Yeah, I saw you guys out there. Going to be hard to beat if you keep that up."

"Thanks, Man. You're in the Singles Division?"

"Yeah."

"I'll try to get over to catch your ride."

"Yeah, do that. Maybe we can all catch up after."

"Sounds good."

When Junior walked away, Jordan gave me a playful shove

"Dude, he don't know it yet, but we're going to make it impossible to beat." Grinning, we picked up our boards and walked back over to the waterline. When our next heat rolled around, I was so amped. There was a clarity to my thoughts, a calmness in my core. I was here to surf, to prove something to myself more than anyone else.

Paddling out, I felt like I was gliding over the water. The ocean had a rhythm, and I was in sync with it. Each wave that came my way seemed like a personal invitation, challenging me to show what I was made of. As I caught wave after wave, nailing each turn and each aerial, I could feel it—all the pieces coming together. My body and mind were in perfect harmony, each movement a precise execution of years of practice and instinct. I was pushing my limits, going for higher aerials and sharper turns.

The crowd's energy was infectious, their cheers pushing me to new heights. I could hear Jordan's whoops of encouragement over the roar of the waves. We were in this together, each of us feeding off the other's performance.

In my third and last heat of the morning, I let loose. It was go big or paddle home. I spotted it on the horizon—a monster wave, towering and formidable. A challenge I couldn't resist. I paddled with all my might, feeling the wave lift me up, up, and up.

I was at its mercy but also in control. I climbed to its peak, feeling the power of the ocean beneath me. I cut back sharply, spraying a fan of water behind me. The crowd's gasp was audible, their excitement palpable. Then came the moment for the big move—an aerial. I launched myself off the lip of the wave, soaring above the water. For a second, it was just me and the sky. The board was an extension of my will, and as I spun in the air, I felt like I could fly. Landing back on the wave, time snapped back into focus. The cheers of the crowd erupted thunderous acclaim. I rode the wave to the end, my heart pounding with adrenaline and victory.

Paddling back to the lineup, I caught Jordan's eye. He was grinning ear to ear, pride and camaraderie in his expression. If the crowd was anything to go by, we weren't just participating; we were dominating this event.

The applause was thunderous, a roar to match the sea. As I made my way back to the beach, every cheer was an affirmation. I'd come to prove something, and there it was—in the nods of my fellow competitors, the wide eyes of the fans on the shore, and Jordan's whoop of victory.

"That's how it's done!" Jordan's hand met mine in a high-five that stung with its intensity.

"Just warming up," I said, but the adrenaline was singing in my blood.

Around mid-day, the Challenge was put on pause, leaving us a couple of hours to kill. I rolled back to the hotel, ready for some grub, a rinse, and a serious chill session. I was going to need it. Only the top two teams in each set would compete this evening, and I knew Jordan and I would be back on the line. So far, I haven't seen anyone better than us.

CHAPTER
TWENTY

When we started gathering for the evening heats, the sun hovered over the horizon, casting a warm, golden glow over the Hawaiian coastline.

I'd taken a breather in my hotel room, though I hadn't been able to sleep, and I returned to the beach, ready to take it on. As I approached, I could tell the atmosphere had changed. The energy that had buzzed with anticipation all morning now crackled with a different intensity. The evening heats were always special, bathed in the soft light of the setting sun, and the crowd had gathered to witness the surfers' final push to secure a spot in the competition's next round. The waves had changed, too. The morning's relatively predictable waters had given way to a more challenging surf, and the currents were stronger. It was as if the ocean itself was testing our mettle, pushing us to our limits.

We were in the last set, in the last heat, and already several crews had been eliminated. We were the ones to catch, and though the competition had been fierce, I wasn't very worried. From what I'd seen and from doing the math, with our lead, there was no way the second-place team could catch us. Jordan and I stood on the sand in front of the announcers' platform, waiting for the results of our set. When the announcers gave the final tallies, Jordan and I celebrated with loud whoops of laughter and high-fives. We'd done it. We lived to see another day.

The next day began as soon as the sun began painting the Hawaiian sky with hues of orange, pink, and purple. After Jordan and I had successfully cleared the first day's elimination heats, the thrill of the competition was like a fire burning high within me, and I was even more pumped to get out there and show those youngsters things that most of them had yet to learn. The waves were rolling in, and the beach was alive with the buzz of anticipation. I staked out a spot and waxed my board, taking the extra moments to stretch and focus. As the morning heats got underway, the six teams were again divided into sets, two teams per set, three heats each. We were first up, and feeling strong, we paddled out with determination. Jordan was right with me, and right off the bat, we were riding high. The judges gave us high scores, and I couldn't help but feel a surge of confidence.

The waves were roaring around us, and the sun cast shimmering diamonds on the water's surface. I felt like I was out there all by myself, dancing with the ocean itself. Our opponents were eliminated, and our team scores were climbing. The excitement was palpable. It felt like the world was finally tilting in our favor, and I could almost taste the victory we'd worked so hard for.

But just as I was about to take on a particularly challenging wave, I caught sight of Jordan, and my stomach dropped.

His face was twisted in pain, his brow furrowed, and his eyes squeezed shut like he'd been hit by a sharp blow. His body jerked, and his leg—the one planted on the board—seized up as if gripped by an invisible vice.

I realized something was seriously wrong. Maybe he'd pulled a muscle or worse. I could see the strain in his eyes; his movements were suddenly jerky and uncoordinated. He tried to shift his stance, but his leg wasn't responding. His knee buckled slightly, and he fought to stay upright, but the balance he usually commanded with ease was slipping away. He looked like a boxer trying to stay on his feet after a brutal punch.

Panic flickered in his eyes as he tried to ride out the wave, but it was clear he was struggling. His normally smooth, confident surfing had turned erratic, every movement forced and painful. It was like watching a car veer off course, trying to regain control but knowing a crash was imminent. Jordan grunted, his mouth twisted in a grimace that I could read even from where I was, and his board wobbled beneath him as his rhythm shattered.

The heat had come to an abrupt halt, and I held my breath. A feeling of dread and concern washed over us as we watched him paddle back toward the shore, each stroke slower and more labored. His face was tight with frustration, every pull of his arms showing the effort it took to keep moving forward. Even to me, the shore appeared agonizingly distant. I could see it in his eyes—the fear that maybe this injury was more than just a passing pain, that it might pull him out of the one thing that kept his world together.

I watched helplessly, torn between continuing my own run and going to my friend's aid. The waves suddenly felt hostile, the once-thrilling challenge now overshadowed by the sight of Jordan struggling to stay afloat. But as I grappled with what to do, a loud whistle pierced the air, and a lifeguard on a jet ski sped toward him. Jordan managed to get on board, but he was hunched over, his hands gripping his knee, his face a mask of agony and frustration. The jet ski carried him away, and as it disappeared from view, a knot of worry tightened in my stomach.

Jordan was my brother in every sense of the word—my partner, my anchor—and seeing him like that hit me hard. He was the toughest guy I knew, someone who had clawed his way up from nothing to become a force in the surf world. For him, surfing wasn't just a sport; it was a lifeline. Without it, everything he'd built for himself and his family back home was at risk. And now, here he was, sidelined and vulnerable, with a messed-up knee that threatened to take away everything he'd fought so hard to achieve.

The announcer blew his whistle and announced the next heat. His voice jolted me back to reality, reminding me that the clock was ticking and the competition was still on. I shook my head, trying to dispel the cloud of anxiety.

I had to keep us in the running, for both of us. I paddled back into position, my arms mechanically slicing through the water. The next wave rose, a towering mass of energy. I hesitated for a fraction of a second, Jordan's accident flashing in my mind. But then something shifted inside me. This was what we trained for, what we lived for. Surfing wasn't just a sport; it was a testament to our resilience and our courage to face the unpredictable nature of the ocean.

With a deep breath, I paddled into the wave, feeling its power lift me. I stood up on my board, every muscle and sinew tensed, ready. I surfed with a new intensity, a blend of fear, determination, and respect for the ocean. Each turn was precise, each maneuver a defiance of the odds. As I rode, I felt I was surfing for both of us now. Each successful ride was a tribute to our partnership and our shared dreams. The crowd's cheers seemed distant, muffled by the rush of blood in my ears. My focus was singular—to surf like it was the last time, to honor the journey we had embarked on together. When the heat ended, I paddled back to shore, exhausted but resolute. I had kept us in the game, but the victory was bittersweet. As I stepped onto the sand, my eyes searched for Jordan. I needed to know he was okay, that we were still a team, no matter what.

As soon as I could, I hurried to the hotel to check on Jordan. He'd been taken to the medics associated with the competition, who confirmed what I had feared—a severe muscle strain in his calf, with the possibility of a partial tear. He was lucky it wasn't worse, but it was bad enough to sideline him. They recommended rest and possibly skipping the evening heats, but Jordan, being Jordan, was too stubborn to listen.

We ate lunch in his room, and though we talked strategy, the air was heavy with unspoken tension. Jordan tried to put on a brave face, but I could see the pain in his eyes every time he moved his leg. He was worried too—not just about the injury, but about letting me down. He knew I was shouldering more of the burden now and that if he wasn't able to perform, it could cost us the competition.

"Jordan, are you sure about this?" I asked, watching him wince as he adjusted his leg on the bed.

"I'm sure," he replied, his voice firm but lacking its usual energy. "I'm not letting you go out there alone. We've come too far for that."

I wasn't convinced, but I knew better than to argue. I just hoped he could manage enough to keep us in the running without making his injury worse.

When it was time to return to the beach, I knocked on his door, and he opened it, swinging it wide so he could haul his surfboard out. He nodded, and I nodded back, and leaving the hotel together we walked down to the competitor's area.

The competitors had been whittled down by another third, and Jordan and I exchanged a nod. We had come through the morning heats but not unscathed. Jordan wasn't a hundred percent by anyone's measure and appeared to still be dealing with whatever had happened to him earlier. I had to be on point tonight if we were going into the championship round tomorrow. I would give all I had and pull out every trick I knew, but I couldn't take his ride for him. I just hope he would be able to do enough without killing himself.

He and I split up on the line so that he and I weren't doing our runs at the same time. He went first, and I watched him like a hawk. He was favoring his leg more than usual, but he'd played it safe and had a decent run. When it was my turn, my mind slid into the zone and my board became an extension of me. I could hear the announcers calling my name, their voices carrying over the water, but they became a part of the white noise— the roar of the water, the pounding of my heart. I let my mind and my body lead the dance as I got into position for the next wave. As the powerful wave surged, I stood, came off the crest and slid in through the back door of the massive cavern of the barrel. Inside, it was timeless and pristine, blue water and white light, the roar of the water like a speeding jet breaking the sound barrier. It was also a Zen moment, peaceful and serene, and I reached out to touch the water as it cupped and rolled over my head.

Entranced, I emerged to bright sunshine, the sparkling ocean, and the screams of the fans and announcers. I blinked, the bright sunshine blinding, riding the tail end of the surge until it broke in waist-deep water. Realizing what I'd just accomplished, I threw my hands up and my head back in jubilation.

"Yes," I screamed, adrenaline surging through every part of me, and I leaped from my board into the rolling wash. I swung my board up out of the water, clutched it tight to my body with one hand, and slogged through the receding water toward the beach. Rivulets of saltwater ran down my face, stinging my eyes, finding their way into my open mouth and down my chin. I shook my head, flinging the water and hair off my face.

People surged around me like an ocean wave, clapping me on my back, shoulders, and arms, shouting and throwing Shakas my way, but when Jordan came up behind me, he grabbed me in a bear hug, practically lifting me off my feet.

"That was as perfect a ride as any I've ever seen," Jordan shouted, his excitement contagious. "That had to be a perfect ten!"

The final day of competition began at seven a.m.. I'd been awake for hours and had even put in a full four-mile run before breakfast. The final men's event wouldn't get underway until much later, after the other divisions had run their heats. I had time on my hands. I'd been going the whole time, in back-to-back heats, and this was the first time I had an opportunity to chill and watch others compete. The Women's and Junior Men's finals were scheduled for the morning and I claimed a seat in the spectator stands to watch. Jordan had stayed in his room at the hotel, and I hoped that he was resting up.

That evening, Jordan had come out to join me. There were only eight of us left in the Men's doubles division, the final four teams to compete for the top prize, and as we stood in the competitor's area, there was a kind of quiet intensity in the air, a shared understanding that this was the moment we had all been working towards. The ocean stretched out before us, and I took a deep breath, letting the salt-tinged air fill my lungs, and I closed my eyes for a moment. This was it—and I was glad. I had come a long way, both as a surfer and as a person, and I was grateful for every step of the journey that had brought me here. With a final glance at the waves, I waded into the water, feeling the familiar coolness embrace my legs. The ocean whispered promises of challenges and triumphs, and I was ready to answer its call.

Today, I would ride these waves with everything I had, not to prove anything to anyone because I believed I had already done that, but simply because it was who I had become—a surfer who found solace, strength, and joy in dancing on the ocean.

I paddled out to the lineup beside Jordan, who looked calm and focused, and anticipation vibrated through every inch of me. I was ready to shine. I was first up, and I watched patiently as the waves rolled in, each a work of art in its own right. Then I saw it. It rose on the horizon, a towering wall of water, and I knew that this would be the moment and the dance. I felt it with all of my being. With a surge of adrenaline, I paddled hard, feeling the water rise beneath me, propelling me forward. The wave grew closer, and I could hear its thunderous roar, a sound that was both terrifying and exhilarating. But I was in my element, a part of the ocean, and I knew that this was where I belonged. As it approached, I turned my board and began to paddle into it. The feeling was electric, the rush of the water beneath me, the power of the ocean lifting me. I could feel every muscle in my body working in perfect harmony, every movement precise and calculated.

And then, I was on it—the wave. Time seemed to slow as I rode the face of the ocean, the world around me a blur of blue and white. The wave was a living, breathing entity, and I was one with it, dancing on its surface as if we were old friends. I carved my board with precision, each turn a testament to years of practice and dedication. The wave carried me, and it was the ride of a lifetime, a moment of pure perfection. The judges on the beach would have no choice but to award me the highest score, but that wasn't what mattered. What mattered was the feeling—the rush of the ride, the connection to the ocean, the knowledge that I had pushed myself to the limit and come out on the other side. As the wave began to close out, I launched myself into the air, performing a final maneuver that left me breathless and exhilarated.

Soon after, I was back in the water, paddling out to the line-up once more, a sense of contentment washing over me. I had done it—I had experienced the perfect ride, a moment of pure bliss and accomplishment. As I looked out at the endless hori-zon, I couldn't help but smile, grateful for every wave, every challenge, and every triumph that had brought me to this point in my life.

That evening, the competitors and Challenge promoters gathered in the hotel ballroom for dinner and the awards pro-gram. Three men and two women sat at the head table on a dais in the front of the room, and the rest of us sat at the round-top tables in front of them. The ballroom was beautifully decorated with gorgeous hibiscus, plumeria, orchids, bird of paradise, and Ti leaves, all abundantly displayed in the floral arrangements around the room.

Jordan and I sat at a table that was only partially full. Our dinner partners were from the Men's and Women's Individuals competitions. We made small talk, sipping drinks until dinner was served. Dinner was American fare this time, roasted chick-en, steak and grilled salmon, rather than the traditional Hawaiian dishes, and I know I wasn't the only one glad that the program ran concurrently with the meal. The MC began with brief but numerous introductions of the five people on the dais, and the awarding of the prizes began immediately after, according to the classifications. The first was for beach lifeguard knee-boarding and moving up through the other skill categories, including bodyboarding, and longboard tow-in. Dessert was being served by the time they'd got to the Men's division and Men's Doubles. Since there were only four teams that had faced off in the finals, the MC called the fourth team up to receive their check. We'd come in third, and Jordan and I went up to receive our prize. The second team and then the winning team came up on the dais to a spate of applause from the audience. We all mugged for the official photographer, holding our envelopes in front of us, while the winning team held up their trophies, and the program ended soon after, the official wrap-up to three days of rigorous, demanding competition.

A reception room had been reserved for us to celebrate the end of the competition. Live music had been arranged and most everyone headed over to party after dinner. Instead of joining the party or returning to my room right away, I joined a few of the people I'd come to know gathered near the bar on the hotel lanai. They were sipping drinks and shooting the breeze. I got a beer and grabbed a seat. We entertained one another with stories about our experiences, swapping stories of the waves, the challenges, the moments of triumph and defeat. Though still recovering from his injury, Jordan managed to put on a smile.

"I may not have been at my best this weekend, but I wouldn't have wanted to compete alongside anyone else. Quinn surfed like Poseidon had touched him, and he pulled it out for us."

Everybody followed up with, "Yeah, brah! Yewww!" and I raised my bottle of beer. "Dude, we totally gave it our all, and that's what really counts, ya know?" Our friends joined in, celebrating everyone's accomplishments.

It was sometime after midnight as our group, which had grown larger the later it got, gradually began to disperse. Some headed to their rooms for rest before their flights, and others lingered to soak in the last moments of our Hawaiian adventure. Feeling a sense of contentment, I bid my friends goodbye and made my way back to my room. My duffel bag, clothes, and gear were tossed in piles around the room. My surfboards were zipped inside their travel cases, standing upright in the closet.

"Gah," I sighed as I began the torturous task of gathering everything up. I hated packing.

I had an early flight out the next morning, and I'd intended to get all my stuff packed and catch some shuteye until I needed to hustle to the airport. It didn't take as long as usual since I'd only brought three days of clothes for socializing and the essentials I needed for the Challenge. A hot shower and sleep were calling my name when someone knocked on my bedroom door. Thinking it might have been Jordan, I went over and swung it open wide, a big grin on my face. Instead of my pal, a short, older man in slacks and a bold Hawaiian shirt stood there, grinning back at me and pushing a business card toward me.

"Quinn Lawler?"

"Who wants to know?" I asked, stifling a yawn.

"Oh, yes. My name's Andy Simpson, and I'm a scout for Copley Talent Management. I know it's a little late, but I saw you leave your friends downstairs, and I was hoping to get a minute of your time. We can talk downstairs if you'd like. I can buy you a drink."

I accepted the business card he was shoving at me and looked at it. I hadn't heard of the Copley Agency before, but it didn't hurt to hear his spiel.

"Downstairs sounds good. Give me a minute. I was packing up my stuff." I closed the door, grabbed my wallet and room keycard, and met him in the hall by the elevators. As we rode down to the lobby, he introduced himself and the reason for stopping by my room. Exiting the elevator, I noticed the lobby was still pretty full, but it seemed that most people were talking in small, hushed groups. I followed Mr. Simpson to a small, out-of-the-way table.

"So, Quinn, it's really great to finally meet you in person. I've been following your performances on the waves all weekend and looked you up on social media and let me tell you, you're good. You've got a talent that's rare to see these days. Your style, your dedication, it's something special. Let me ask you a question, though. How come you're surfing the Challenge? You guys just finished up in Banyu Wangi, Indonesia, in September, and before that, you were carving it up in Tahiti."

"Fair question, Andy. I'm thinking of riding solo, maybe

even pulling a team together."

"Yeah, okay, I understand. You're still young. You got time on your side."

"Uhm, well, that's good to know."

"We can help you. We know what it takes to make it big in the surfing world. We're not just about finding sponsorships, you know. Copley's about building brands, your brand. I mean, you know, not just competing in the biggest surf competitions but being the face of them. We're talking endorsements, media exposure, training with the best coaches, and access to top-tier equipment. We have a global network and plenty of industry know-how. We can open doors for you that others can't. Just think about it, Quinn. Think bigger than just surfing; think about becoming a surfing icon. I see potential in you not just as a surfer but as a personality that can inspire the next generation."

"Yo, you see me cheesing it up for the cameras?"

"Yeah, why not? Now, I know this is a big decision, and Copley's gonna want you to feel 100% about it. I want you to feel 100% about it. So, let's kick around what you want from your surfing career, and I'll show you how Copley's can help get you there. How does that sound?"

It sounded great, except I hadn't really spun my life or a surfing career that far out. It had taken me days agonizing over the decision to come here and surf in the team events with Jordan. I didn't even sign up for the single. Yeah, it sounded really good, but I wasn't ready to go that far just yet. Yeah, I knew how this worked. I had expected to be approached by the scouts and pressured to sign on the dotted line, but that was Jordan's dream, not necessarily mine. Still, we sat and talked for about half an hour. He gave me some good pointers and a few ideas began to bubble in my brain, but I told him to give me a few days before I'd get back to him. He was really cool about not making the sale, shook my hand, and I left him in the lobby, looking around for another prospect. It was two a.m., and I had a nine o'clock fight to catch. I needed some shuteye.

CHAPTER TWENTY-ONE

I arrived at LAX late in the afternoon and got a rideshare to take me back to San Nobel.

I knew Harry would come pick me up, but he'd have to close up shop to do it and get caught up in LA's traffic snarl coming and going. However, I could hardly wait to see him and tell him everything. I was even pumped with excitement to tell him about the Copley Agency and the meeting with the talent scout, though I wasn't sure I wanted to go down that road. Still, It was nice to be touted. However, before I could even think about their offer, I needed to check them out. Maybe even call Vince or Jeff to see if they'd ever heard of them. Thinking about it, I probably needed to give all the guys a call, including Josh and Sean, to see how they were doing. As Josh had said, "We were still family, weren't we?"

The ride home cost me a hundred dollars because I gave the driver a nice tip. But it was worth it. I was excited to celebrate with Harry, Joanna, and everyone at the Shack. When I stepped through the front door, rather than the back door, the crowd went wild. Well, Harry was happy to see me. Mr. Jacobson hailed me from his seat at a table by the wall, a basket of shrimp tacos in front of him. And a couple of people who worked at the shops on the boardwalk were there, happy to see me as well.

"How did it go, Kid?" Harry asked, giving me a big hug and a couple of pats on the back.

"Good, Harry. We got third overall after a few mishaps. It was a nice showing and a decent check. How've you been?"

"Hustling around here. Must've gone soft while you were here." He did look a bit haggard, maybe a little older than he was just five days ago, and a lot more tired. I didn't know how old Harry was, but since most of his hair had gone white, I just figured he was probably a senior citizen or close to it.

"You need a hand back there?" I asked, going behind the counter to the back. "I couldn't get back before the rush, but I can help clean up." I stopped in the center of the room and stared. Every pot and pan had to be dirty and stacked in every available space.

"Wow, it was busy, wasn't it?" I quipped, but Harry didn't say anything. I grabbed a clean apron, tied it around my waist, rolled up my sleeves, and ran hot water and soap in the sink. Depending on how long the pots and pans, dishes, glassware, and silverware had been sitting, I figured I could knock it all out with no sweat. Customers trickled in until the sun began to set, and Harry took care of them while asking me at least a thousand-and-one questions about Hawaii, the luau and the Kalua pig, and the Challenge. I ended up explaining what 'mishaps' occurred for Jordan and me to barely snag third place, and he wanted to know how it felt crushing the Hawaiian waves. We kept a running Q and A going until the last dish, pot, pan, glass and fork were clean and put away. Harry sat on a tall stool he kept in the kitchen and talked to me while I straightened the shelves in the pantry, doing inventory as I went along. It was fully dark when Harry locked up the Shack.

"Thanks, Quinn. It probably would've taken me all evening to clean up. Can't keep up when the lunch rush slams me."

"Well, I'm back now, Harry. You want a beer? I think I still have a couple in the fridge."

"Nah, I need to get on home, take my pills and put my feet up. Doc says I've got high blood pressure, so she put me on a diet and wants me to exercise. Who has time for exercise?"

"We can make time for you to exercise, Harry. Are you okay? I mean, really okay? I know you've been seeing the doctor kinda regularly, but I've never heard you talk about taking medicine and stuff like that before."

"I'm fine, just getting old. Have fun while you're young, Kiddo. Getting old is for the birds. The doctors give you all kinds of pills, but nothing stops time. Good night, Quinn."

"Night, Harry."

I waited and watched as he backed the car out of the garage and onto the street. With a wave, he pulled off, and I went upstairs. Something felt amiss. Harry wasn't sharing the whole story with me.

The next morning, I skipped going out on the waves and opened up the Shack for Harry. I swept and mopped the floors, wiped down all the tables and chairs, and put on the coffee. Harry came in, looking much better after a good night's sleep and seemed more like his usual self. We fell into our natural rhythm, him cooking up the orders while I served, busing down the tables, and cleaning up in the back. We'd long ago stop worrying about my hours, and I was working about as long as Harry. I wasn't concerned about a paycheck, living rent free was worth more than every cent Harry tried to scratch out for me every week. Since I'd come home, a couple of ideas had been brewing in the back of my mind, but before I could make them happen, I had to make a couple of calls first.

After work the next afternoon, I decided to sit down and create a plan. I planned to go back on the circuit. It was what I knew best, and instead of scratching the itch, the Aloha Challenge only made it more maddening, like when the palm of your hand itched, and no matter how much you scratched and rubbed it, it didn't go away until it went away on its own. The circuit was that kind of itch. But if I was gone, and I would be gone a lot, Harry would be here by himself, getting slammed every day with the lunch rush, and soon the summer crowds would be back. He wasn't looking too good, moving around a little slower, though he could still handle the grill and fryers. I'd be worried about leaving everything on his shoulders. Although I had little input in what Harry did with the Shack, I'd be bereft and pretty much set adrift again if he closed it up or sold it.

The only course of action would be to help him out. The Shack could use some refreshing. Maybe expand it a few feet to give it more room in the kitchen and dining room, infuse it with some fresh personality, and then hire staff to help out in the kitchen, rotating their hours to give Harry a break and work the dining room. In my mind, I began to see the Shack transform, looking more like the bar and grill I was used to hanging out in. I seriously doubted Harry would go for a massive transformation, but if he went along with half the ideas spinning around in my brain, he'd be making money hands over fist, and he wouldn't have to do everything himself. I'd do some homework on that, and when I got it together, I'd see how he felt about it. Money was not going to be the biggest problem with this project.

The next thing was figuring out how I could get back on the surf circuit on a shoestring budget. I could blow all my money on travel and entry fees, food and hotel and not get a cent back in prize money. I needed sponsors. I needed boards and other gear—things I took for granted when Josh was footing the team's bills. I needed a PA like Josh's Monica to keep my schedule, arrange flights, and keep me on time for meetings and promos that I needed to attend. Sponsors footed a lot of the bills so I could rep their merchandise. That's some of what talent agencies like that guy, Andy what's-him-name at that Copley Talent Agency was talking about. I looked them up, but there wasn't much to be found. Only in business for a few years, no big roster of clients or affiliates. I suddenly remembered what Josh had told me the day the world fell apart.

"Call me any time you need something, Quinn. It doesn't matter what or when, how much or how little. We might not be a team anymore, but we're still family." And I'd promised him I would. Well, this seemed like a good time to call him up. I needed some advice and maybe some help. I hit his mobile number and waited for it to ring. He picked up on the first ring.

"Quinn, Buddy, how are you? Doing good, yeah?" I grinned, hearing his voice. He sounded happy to hear from me.

"Yeah, Josh, yeah. Doing real good. How about you? What have you been up to?"

"Hanging with family mostly, Sean sometimes. Been working on a couple of ideas…next steps you know? How about you?"

"Same. I took a little break from the circuit myself for a while, then Jordan and I hooked up and surfed Hawaii, the North Shore. We just got back. Got third in the men's doubles; the prizes weren't too shabby."

"Good, good. Some of the boys were at the Cape a few weeks ago. Heard they were shredding it up. I try to keep tabs on all of you, but I haven't heard any news about you and Jordan. So, tell me, what else is going on?"

"Well, I've got a question for you. While I was in Hawaii, I was approached by an agent from Copley Talent Management Group. Wondering if you ever heard of them." He was quiet on the line for a long minute, which I assumed meant he was thinking so I gave him space.

"No, haven't heard of them, but I've been locked in with our sponsors so long, I never kept up with any of the other agencies. You looking to get sponsored, Quinn? You want to go back on the circuit?"

"Yeah. I'm ready to do it, Josh."

"Okay, that's good. I'll make some calls on your behalf. Maybe I can interest some of our old sponsors. Okay?"

"Yeah, yeah, man, that would be cool. I was chasing my tail, trying to figure out how to make things happen. Thanks, man. I appreciate anything you can do."

"No worries, Quinn. Pick up your training routine so you're ready when they start calling, okay? And I'll get back to you in a couple of days, yeah?"

"Yeah, cool, Josh. I'll be ready when they start calling. I'm ready now."

"I know, buddy. You always had discipline. Where are you? Text me your address."

"I'm in San Nobel, California."

"California? I would have guessed you'd be in the south of France or somewhere. Where's San Nobel?"

"A little ways north of LA. My address should be coming through now."

"I got it. Did you stay in California after we left?

"Yeah. I got family here."

"Yeah, I forgot you're a SoCal boy. Look, I gotta take a call. We'll talk in a couple of days. Don't worry, you'll be okay."

When we hung up, I could swear I was floating on clouds. In less than ten minutes, Josh had set my world right. He had the connections and was willing to call on them for me. He had faith in me and was willing to back me. I leaped off the futon with a loud whoop, punching the air with my fist. Damn straight, I'd be ready when they start calling. I was ready now, but I'd be spit shined when people started dropping on the beach trying to scope me out.

I needed to get back on my nutrition routine and stop eating so much fried food in the Shack, so I borrowed Harry's car and drove downtown. I stocked up on everything I needed. I made a stop at the market for some fresh vegetables, lean meat, beans, and grains. I knew what I needed, but I was going to need Harry's help to prepare most of it. Most of the time, we'd had a trained chef who traveled with the team, and we'd all eaten together. This was going to be a learning experiment for both Harry and me. I also picked up a clean-eating cookbook to help us along.

Finished with my shopping, I texted Joanna, offering coffee and pie at Patty's diner. As soon as the text was sent, I shook my head. Neither coffee nor pie was on the clean eating menu. I sighed. Turning my stomach around was going to take some time and effort. Fortunately, she pleaded for a rain check. She wouldn't get off until six, and she needed to go home and check on her mom afterward. In the midst of my excitement, I'd forgotten today was the nurse's evening off, and Joanna took care of her mother. I texted her back.

"Call me when you get settled. Got lots of news to share."

She sent back a thumbs-up emoji.

CHAPTER
TWENTY-TWO

On Sunday afternoon, right after the New Year, Joanna and I took a walk along the beach.

We held hands like teenagers as we walked. Every so often, I would kick a stray piece of driftwood, lost in thought. As if sensing my preoccupation, she nudged me gently.

"You're awfully quiet. What's going on?"

I glanced at her, the ocean breeze tousling her dark brown hair. "I've been thinking about Harry… and the Shack," I began, watching the waves lap gently at the shore. "The place has so much character, but it could really use some sprucing up. I've been toying with the idea of renovating it for him."

Joanna's eyes lit up with interest. "That sounds like a fantastic idea! Harry would love that. What are you thinking?"

"Well, I don't know that he'd love it, but the kitchen definitely needs some updating. Maybe some new appliances, better storage solutions," I said, envisioning the cramped space where Harry worked his magic. "And the dining area could be more inviting. New tables, maybe some local art on the walls, expanding it for more seating…"

She walked alongside me, listening intently. "You know, it really could use livening. Maybe create a dinner menu, not just sandwiches, you know? People love to have dinner outside by the beach."

I nodded, appreciating her input. "Yeah, that's a great idea. We could add a deck area, maybe, looking out at the ocean. It would change the whole vibe of the place. I had an upscale bar-and-grill-type vibe in mind. Neon lights, beachy kind of paraphernalia on the walls…."

We reached our favorite small cove, where the sound of the waves was more pronounced. I stopped and leaned against the bluff wall and pulled her in front of me, standing in between my feet. We looked out at the ocean, and I let the vision for the Shack bloom in my mind.

"Harry's done so much for me. He gave me a place to stay, a job, and, more importantly, a sense of belonging when I was pretty lost. I want to give something back, you know?"

Joanna turned in my arms and faced me, her expression soft. "I think it's wonderful, Quinn. It's a way to show Harry how much he means to you. And you know, I'd be more than happy to help." I smiled at her, feeling a wave of gratitude for her support.

"Thanks. That means a lot. We could turn the Shack into something really special. A place that not only serves great food but a place for people to come out and enjoy themselves."

"But doing a big renovation project like you're thinking could add up pretty quickly and take months, not a few weeks. Expanding means knocking down walls and putting up new ones, and you'd need permits from the city. I doubt you and Harry would be able to do much work yourselves."

"Heck no. We'd need a design and construction company. Probably an architect to draw up the floor plan and stuff." I kicked at the sand, feeling a mix of determination and uncertainty. We might be able to get a loan at the bank. I'd secure it, then pay it off. I haven't told Harry, nor you for that matter, but I'm going back on the surf circuit. The captain of my old team is helping me secure sponsors and an agent I can trust. I intend to hire staff so Harry won't have to work so hard."

"You care so much for Harry, Quinn. It's really touching, you know. They say people come into your life for a reason or a season, and sometimes, f you're lucky, they'll be there for a lifetime. Harry's lucky you found him."

"I think I'm the lucky one. Besides, I'm a little selfish too. I need someplace to call home in between surf events. You and San Nobel and Harry and the Shack all feel like home. I don't know what would happen to me if Harry closed up shop or sold it off."

"I wouldn't want to imagine what would happen to him, either."

"Yeah. We both need the Shack. But it needs a little work."

"I assume you haven't talked to him at all about it...."

"No, I needed to have it all worked out first. Give him something to agree to. I got some preliminary numbers, and I'm looking at anywhere from one-hundred-twenty-five-thousand to upwards of two-hundred-eighty. I'm not sure Harry will go for those kinds of numbers." The idea of diving into this project with her was reassuring, yet the financial aspect was like a looming wave, ready to crash. I didn't want to dive in blindly and end up in over my head financially.

Joanna seemed thoughtful. "There are definitely ways to keep costs down, like doing some of the work yourself, but if you are away surfing while construction is going on, you'll need someone to stay on to oversee the work and the numbers. I can help with the budget, make sure costs don't get out of hand, and source materials locally."

"That would be great. I want to do this for Harry, and for me. I need to get all my facts and numbers straight before I approach him."

We started walking again, and as we neared the front of the Shack, I stopped and looked out at the ocean, a place that had always brought me clarity.

"If it's okay, let's sit inside, look at the numbers, and figure out a plan. I want to make sure we do this right."

Joanna squeezed my hand, her support unwavering. "Sounds like a plan. It can work, Quinn, and it doesn't have to break the bank….pun intended."

I laughed at her silly pun, and we headed up to my place. I'd stacked all the brochures and papers with floor plans and projections on the kitchen counter to keep things orderly, and we spread them out on the dining table. I knew them backward and forward by heart, and I waited for Joanna to look them over. She flipped through them slowly, her finger tracing the new floor plans.

"You were right, Quinn. Expanding could really transform it. More space for more customers, and there could be different zones—like a larger casual dining area for families and an additional relaxed bar section."

"Yeah," I said, excited that she could also see my vision. "That could really set us apart, make this place a destination not just for the food but also for the experience. People love experiences and good vibes." Joanna nodded enthusiastically. "Exactly! You could keep the cozy, rustic feel inside but elevate it. Better lighting, comfortable seating, and maybe, as you said, some coastal art and artifacts on the walls. Not that kitschy stuff, but real surfboards and stuff."

Our ideas were flowing now, melding, each one building on the last.

"We should also consider a menu refresh," I suggested. "Keep the classics that everybody loves, bring in a real chef and add some new, exciting dishes. Maybe play up the clean eating angle."

As we talked, the vision of the Shack's future started to take shape in my mind. It was ambitious, maybe even a bit daunting, but it felt right. This wasn't just about renovation; it was about creating something new, something that reflected both the history of the place and the potential of what it could become. Harry would still own it and run it, but he'd have a lot of help. I'm sure he'd see the benefit in that.

It was late when Joanna left. I'd tried to entice her to stay the night, but she would hear of it. It's grown closer during the Christmas holidays, deepening our relationship to include spending nights together. Sometimes, I could get her to stay, but most nights, she'd have to leave before it got too late. Her mother had round-the-clock care, but Joanna felt uncomfortable leaving her mother overnight. I understood perfectly and was just happy that she came over as much as she did and stayed as long as she could.

CHAPTER
TWENTY-THREE

The afternoon rush finally dwindled, leaving a rare moment of quiet. When I approached him, Harry was behind the counter, methodically cleaning up.

"You got a second, Harry? There's something I've been thinking about, and I wanted to run it by you." Harry looked up, his hands pausing in their work.

"Sure, Kid, what's on your mind?"

"Let's go sit over there," I said, pointing at a table in the dining room. He nodded and followed me over. I flipped the sign to the side that read Closed, will be back shortly and pulled all the papers I'd brought with me, spreading them in front of him.

"What's all of this?" He asked. "This is the Shack?" he asked, holding up a blueprint of the new floor plan.

I took a deep breath. The ideas and numbers I had been juggling suddenly felt more real. "I've been thinking about the Shack, you know, about how much potential it has, and I want to invest in it. I've got some money saved and we could expand and renovate it and turn it into a real money-maker. Like a bar and grill or a modern café. Have you ever thought about doing that, Harry?" I looked earnestly at the man in front of me imploringly, and he settled back in his chair, a thoughtful look crossing his weathered face. "Expand the Shack, huh? I'd thought about it once or twice, but to do something worthwhile was a big undertaking. Why are you thinking about doing it, Quinn?"

"I want to do it for you...and for me."

I laid out the ideas Joanna and I had brainstormed—expanding the dining area, updating the kitchen, adding a bar and possibly an outdoor patio, and hiring plenty of help. I also told him that I was going back on the circuit, taking part in the World Masters Championship in Montañita, Ecuador in five weeks.. He understood it was who I was and what I was meant to do, and I now had a lot of people in my corner, including him and Joanna.

"I know it's a lot," I continued, "I plan to surf and renovating this place won't be all that quick or cheap. But I think it could really turn this place into something even more special. I've even started looking into the costs. But don't think I'm just going to go back on the circuit and disappear from around here, Harry. I intend to come back after every event to check on you, the Shack, and my little, tiny studio apartment over the garage. This is my life, Harry. You gave me the chance to get myself together, and I'm ready to do what I'm supposed to be doing."

I didn't say that I needed it all in my life—surfing, Harry and Joanna, and the Shack. I didn't have to tell him I wasn't ready to turn any one of the loose. But I could tell that Harry had listened, even though his expression was unreadable, even though he didn't say a word. He understood. And I knew I would get an earful one day while we'd be in the kitchen getting slammed during the rush when he thought I wouldn't remember this conversation. It was his way, and I wouldn't have it any other way.

When I finally shut up, one corner of his mouth lifted in a half smile that lasted about two seconds. Then he looked at me, wiping his hands on his apron.

"I appreciate the thought, Quinn. I really do. But you know this Shack... it's been my life since I left the Marines. Changing it is no small decision."

"I know," I replied quickly, "and I wouldn't want to do anything you're not comfortable with. This place... it's become a home to me. I see so much potential here. And I want to help make it happen, financially too."

Harry's eyes studied me, and there was a softness in them. "You've really thought this through, haven't you?"

"Yeah. I even got a line of credit at the bank to cover the renovations." I hadn't since I'd intended to pay for them myself, but he would balk again if I told him that. "It's like a secured loan."

"You'd be an investor or a partner?"

"Whichever you'd be comfortable with," I said quickly. I hadn't really figured out the difference, but I think I would prefer being a partner to just being an investor. I wasn't looking to recoup my money right away. I wanted the place to succeed so I'd have it to call home.

He made a sound that was a grunt and a chuckle combined. "Give me some time to think about it. It's a big step, but maybe... maybe it's time for a change."

I nodded, feeling a mix of relief and anticipation. "Of course, take all the time you need. I just want you to know that I want to do this for the both of us." I scooped everything together, and slid them into the folder I'd brought them in and handed them to Harry.

"These are for you to look over. Feel free to change anything you want. Nothing is set in stone."

"Thanks, Kid," he said, and in those two words, I heard how much this place meant to him, the years and the security that had come from standing behind that counter, day in and day out. I nodded and left, giving him time and space to mull over what a more upscale Seafood Shack could look like.

A few days later, I came down ready to get the morning going and found Harry woolgathering as he sat, sipping his coffee.

"Morning, Quinn," he said as I came in the door. "Got a minute?"

"Of course," I said, coming to stand next to him with a mix of anticipation and nervousness, and he turned to me, his eyes meeting mine.

"I've been thinking about what you said the other day. About fixing up the Shack." He paused, taking another sip of his coffee. I nodded. I hadn't brought the subject up anymore, giving him all the time he needed to decide what he wanted to do. "Well, I'm in. Let's go for it. But I don't want you on the hook for all of the money. I have pretty decent credit. I can go in on the loan with you. We'll be partners. Fifty-one percent for me, forty-nine for you. How's that?"

Relief and excitement surged through me. "Really? That's great, Harry! I've got a bunch of ideas I've been working on with Joanna."

Harry nodded, setting his coffee down. "I've been thinking, too. If we're doing this, let's do it right. First off, the kitchen. I agree we need to modernize it—get better appliances, a more efficient layout, and more storage. All of that. It's the heart of the Shack, after all."

I eagerly agreed, "Absolutely, the kitchen's top of the list. And what about the dining area? I was thinking of opening it up, maybe adding some large windows so that we can get the full ocean view...."

"Good idea," Harry mused. "And I like the idea of making the most of our location with a deck stretching from the front and going around both sides. Everybody likes eating outside; we can put up some of those sails instead of umbrellas so people can enjoy their meals al fresco."

"That's exactly what Joanna and I were thinking," I said, excited to see Harry so involved in the vision.

Harry laughed heartily. "You're thinking big, Quinn. Don't get me wrong, though. I like it. But I don't know about making the Shack a fancy restaurant and all. What about our regulars? They love us the way we are. I'm comfortable, too, with the way we are."

I know, Harry." I replied, "We don't have to do a whole lot if you don't want to. I was thinking it might give this place a whole new lease on life. You tell me, Harry, what you want, and we'll do it just like that. Okay?"

Harry stood up, a faraway look on his face. "I know this place is small, but it doesn't have to be, you know. I bought the lots on each side when I bought the Shack. There wasn't much of anything out here then. I had a lot of ideas about what I wanted to do, but I never did anything. You want to make this place into something, Quinn, I'm with you. We can start talking to some companies when you're ready to start." he said, clasping my shoulder.

I've already called around, found a few reasonably priced companies, and talked to some of their references. You can take your pick. I put their brochures in the folder. Maybe this evening, we can crunch some numbers and set up our budget. Joanna's our point person for making sure the financials run smoothly."

"Seems you and Joanna are working pretty close. Got some more news for me?" He asked making me blush, the heat turning my face beet red.

"Not yet, Harry. Maybe soon, but not yet."

"Well, okay, not yet." He chuckled. "Thanks, Quinn. You know I appreciate you thinking about the Shack and me," he said, his voice more serious, "Thank you for caring about this old place as much as I do."

As he walked back to the kitchen, I stood there for a moment, staring into space. This project was more than just a renovation; it was a chance to strengthen the Shack's legacy, and now, with Harry's blessing and guidance, it felt like everything was possible.

CHAPTER
TWENTY-FOUR

The days passed quickly after we closed the Shack for renovations, and soon it was time for my return to the circuit, back with the big boys who knew me by name and knew my stats.

I'd spent weeks preparing, getting myself back into peak condition, and now it was time to see if all that work would pay off. The night before my flight to Montañita, Joanna and I spent the evening together, savoring the last few hours before I had to leave. There was something different in the air between us—something unspoken but heavy with meaning. I could feel it as we lay in bed, her body warm and comforting next to mine. Usually, before a big competition, I'd be focused on strategy, on mentally preparing myself for the waves, but tonight, my thoughts kept drifting back to her.

I turned to look at Joanna, her face soft and relaxed in the dim light. How did I get so lucky? The thought hit me hard, almost out of nowhere. I reached out, tucking a strand of hair behind her ear, and she stirred slightly, her eyes fluttering open.

"Sorry," I whispered. "Didn't mean to wake you."

She smiled, her hand finding mine. "It's okay. You're leaving tomorrow. I'd rather be awake with you than miss out on the time we have left."

Her words tugged at something deep inside me. I wasn't used to this—having someone who cared enough to miss me, who wanted to be with me right up until the last possible minute. It was a feeling I hadn't expected but one I was starting to crave.

"You're going to be amazing out there, Quinn," she said softly, her voice steady despite the emotion I could see in her eyes. "But I'm going to miss you like crazy."

I squeezed her hand, feeling the weight of her words settle in my chest. "I'm going to miss you too," I admitted, my voice rougher than I intended. "But knowing you'll be here when I get back... it makes leaving a little easier."

Joanna's smile was gentle and understanding. "I'll be right here, waiting for you."

The next morning, she helped me carry all my gear downstairs, neither of us saying much. There was no need for words; everything that mattered had already been said. We loaded the bags into the trunk of Harry's car, and I felt a pang of something unfamiliar—something that felt a lot like longing.

Harry was already behind the wheel, beaming with pride. He was like the proud dad seeing his son off to their first big adventure, and I couldn't help but grin back at him. But when I turned to Joanna, standing there with her hand raised in a wave, that grin softened into something else—something deeper.

As Harry pulled away, I leaned out the window, watching her until she was out of sight. I'd never felt so full of love for anyone in my life before. They were my family, and I was determined to do them proud—and, in Harry's case, even prouder if that was even possible.

The flight to Ecuador was long, about ten hours, but it gave me plenty of time to think. I mentally ran through my strategy for the competition, but my thoughts kept circling back to Joanna and Harry. Knowing they were rooting for me made this trip feel different from any other I'd taken. I wasn't just doing this for myself anymore—I was doing it for them too.

When I arrived in Montañita, the familiar rush of excitement hit me like a wave. This was it. I met up with Jordan and some of the guys I knew from my days on the circuit as part of the team. We grabbed dinner, caught up and talked strategy, but all I could think about was getting back out there. My mind kept drifting to the next day, to the ocean that awaited us.

The next morning, the sun was a fiery orb rising over the horizon, casting long shadows on the sand. I stood at the edge of the beach, my board tucked under my arm, the familiar weight grounding me as I looked out at the ocean. The waves rolled in with a steady rhythm, their white crests catching the early light. It felt like coming home. The sound of the waves was like a heartbeat, steady and strong, reminding me of why I was here. I took a deep breath, letting the salty air fill my lungs, and closed my eyes for a moment. This was what I'd been working toward, what I'd been missing. The months of preparation, the early mornings, the grueling workouts—it all led to this.

"Quinn! You ready, man?"

I opened my eyes to see Jordan jogging over, a wide grin on his face. My teammate, my friend. The one who'd stuck by me even when things had gone sideways.

"More than ready," I replied, grinning back. My heart pounded in my chest, not from nerves but from excitement. I was here. I was back. And more than anything, I was ready to prove it to myself.

The buzz of the crowd swelled as more competitors gathered, the energy of the beach building with each passing minute. There was a hum of anticipation in the air, a collective breath being held before the action began. My gaze swept over the other surfers, each one focused, determined. I knew some of them, had ridden waves with a few, and competed against others. But this time felt different. I wasn't just another face in the lineup. I was here to make a statement. This wasn't just about the competition; it was about reclaiming something I'd lost.

The announcer's voice crackled over the loudspeakers, calling the first heat to the water. I felt my pulse quicken as Jordan and I headed to the lineup, the familiar adrenaline rush kicking in. This was the moment I'd been waiting for—the moment to see if all those doubts, all those questions, would be answered. We paddled out, the water cool against our skin, and the world narrowed down to just the waves and the board beneath me.

As the first set approached, I glanced over at Jordan, who gave me a nod. No words were needed. We were in sync, just like we'd been in Hawaii, but this time, there was no injury holding us back. This time, it was about proving we were still contenders.

The wave rose up, and I felt the pull as it began to form, my body reacting instinctively. I paddled hard, feeling the surge of power as the wave lifted me. In that moment, everything else fell away—the noise of the crowd, the pressure, the expectations. It was just me and the wave, the ocean's energy flowing through me. It was like reconnecting with an old friend, one who had been waiting for me all along.

I dropped in, carving a line down the face of the wave, my movements fluid yet precise. The board responded to my every command, slicing through the water as I rode the wave with a mix of power and grace. The rush of wind against my face, the spray of saltwater, the sheer joy of being in my element—it was all there, just like I remembered. But it was more than just muscle memory. It was a reminder that this was where I belonged.

Time seemed to stretch, each second filled with the purest form of freedom I'd ever known. As the wave began to close out, I pulled off an aerial maneuver, launching myself into the air with a burst of energy. The world tilted, and for a brief moment, I was weightless, suspended between sky and sea. In that moment, it wasn't just about the competition; it was about the love of the ride, the connection to the ocean that had never really left me.

I landed cleanly, the board reconnecting with the water as if it had never left. The crowd erupted in cheers, but I barely heard them. I rode the wave all the way to shore, my heart pounding, a grin stretching across my face. This was why I surfed. This was why I'd come back.

As I paddled back out, Jordan caught up to me, his face lit with excitement. "That was sick, man! You've still got it!"

I laughed, the sound carried away by the wind. "Feels like I never left." And in a way, I hadn't. This was where I was meant to be, and I knew it now more than ever.

We finished the heat strong, both of us pushing our limits, riding wave after wave with the kind of intensity that only came from knowing what was at stake. When it was over, we paddled back to the beach, breathless but exhilarated. The ocean had given me everything I needed—confidence, clarity, and the reminder that this was where I belonged.

On shore, the announcer's voice boomed out the results, and I felt a thrill as our names were called—first place in the heat. It was only the beginning, but it was enough to remind me why I was here. I wasn't just back—I was here to stay.

Back at the hotel later that night, after the adrenaline had faded, I sat on the balcony overlooking the ocean. The moon cast a silver path on the water, and the waves rolled in with a soothing rhythm. I knew there would be more challenges ahead and more waves to ride, but tonight, I allowed myself to savor the victory. It wasn't just about winning the heat; it was about proving to myself that I could still do this, that I still had what it took.

Tomorrow, I'd do it all again. And the day after that. Because this is who I am, who I'm meant to be. A surfer. Riding the tides. Chasing the horizon. But now, I've got something more—a place to call home, people who believe in me, and a future that feels as boundless as the ocean before me.

CHAPTER
TWENTY-FIVE

The next few weeks were a blur of plans, permits, and late-night meetings.

Joanna took charge of the financial side, poring over spreadsheets and working her magic to keep costs in check. Harry and I spent countless hours with architects and designers, turning his old dream of a 5-star restaurant into a tangible plan. We pored over blueprints, discussing every detail, from the layout of the kitchen to the positioning of the dining tables. We wanted the new place to have the soul of the Shack but elevated—clean lines, ocean views, and a vibe that whispered sophistication without losing its roots.

When demolition day came, it hit us hard. The Shack wasn't just a building; it was a piece of us, filled with memories of long days, late nights, and the laughter of regulars who had become like family. Watching the walls come down felt like saying goodbye to an old friend. Harry stood by the entrance, his hands deep in his pockets, staring as the first blows of the wrecking ball tore into the old wood. I watched him out of the corner of my eye, seeing the emotions play across his face—a mixture of nostalgia, loss, and a hint of excitement for what was to come.

"This is harder than I thought it'd be," he admitted quietly, his voice thick. "But it's good, you know? It's time."

I nodded, knowing exactly what he meant. The Shack had been a sanctuary, a place of comfort and routine, but it was time for it to evolve, just like we were. We were tearing down walls, but we were building something bigger—something that would carry the legacy forward.

The construction site buzzed with activity, the sound of saws and hammers creating a constant rhythm. Joanna and I worked on every little detail, wanting to ensure the place looked and felt like Harry's dream was brought to life. Watching the transformation was like watching a dream take shape, one brick, one plank at a time. There were setbacks, of course—delays in shipments, budget hiccups, and days when nothing seemed to go right—but through it all, Harry's vision kept us moving forward. The Breakwater was more than a restaurant. It was a tribute to his legacy, to our partnership, and to the community that had supported us from the beginning.

I was winning more of my heats on the circuit than I was losing and being frugal with my money, except for flying home as much as I could. It cost to fly in for a couple of days here and there, but it was worth it to me. And I felt both excited and sad to see all of the changes. The first time I saw the empty lot where the Shack once stood, it was like a physical blow to the chest. I don't know how Harry stood it. So when Joanna mentioned Harry was thinking about attending a reunion with some of his retired buddies from the Marines on Parris Island near Beaufort, South Carolina, I thought it was a great idea, and I made sure he had first-class accommodations.

Coming back home and seeing The Breakwater for the first time felt like stepping into a dream I didn't know I was having. The restaurant rose at the water's edge, its sleek, modern lines cutting against the sky like a promise fulfilled. Floor-to-ceiling windows captured the light, reflecting the ocean onto the polished wood floors inside. The façade, with its blend of reclaimed wood and clean, sophisticated steel, had this rustic yet upscale vibe that made it feel like it had always been there.

I parked at the far end of the lot and just stood there, taking it all in. The last time I saw this place, it was all bones and scaffolding, the promise of what it could be still hanging in the air. Now, it was nearly complete, the building gleaming in the golden hour sun, though I could still hear activity inside.

Joanna had kept me in the dark on purpose, wanting this moment to be a surprise. No updated photos, no sneak peeks—nothing. As I walked toward the entrance, the faint sounds of jazz drifted out, mingling with the rhythm of the waves. It was perfect. It was the kind of place that would make you stop in your tracks and feel like you'd stumbled onto something special.

I ran my hand along the smooth wooden railing of the deck, feeling the quality of the work. Every detail had been designed with care. The outdoor seating area would soon be dotted with cozy tables and shaded by sleek awnings, giving the space a modern yet welcoming feel. Palms, potted plants and other greenery would line the decks and walkways, blurring the lines between the restaurant and the sea. From where I stood, I could see the soft curve of the coastline and the waves rolling in with that familiar rhythm that felt like home.

Inside, the vibe would be elevated but unpretentious—like the best kind of hidden gem. Sophisticated, but not stuffy. Polished wood floors were installed, as were the exceptionally high, wood-beamed ceilings. We still needed to select ocean-inspired artwork to give it an airy, open feel, warm lighting, and maybe some nautical touches. I could imagine Harry inside, moving between the tables, talking to the customers, helping the wait-staff, and checking on the final touches. The thought made my chest tighten. I could imagine how proud he would be.

I walked further inside, and the bar caught my eye.

The bar itself looked as if it had been carved by master craftsmen, a sleek curve of cherry wood that gleamed in the sunlight. Polished mirrors and glass shelves reflected that light that bounced around the room. Soon, the shelves would display high-end spirits and elegant glassware. The expanse of space was completely empty, but I could easily imagine the plush seating we'd picked out creating intimate conversation spaces without sacrificing the ocean views.

Joanna stood at my side, her eyes sparkling with pride. "It's something, isn't it?"

I could only nod, momentarily lost for words. It wasn't just something. It was everything. "This place is… it's incredible," I finally managed, my voice thick with emotion. "You've outdone yourself, Jo."

She laughed, squeezing my hand. "We've all done it. It's everything Harry dreamed of and more. He was the one with the vision."

We walked through the space together, envisioning each space. The kitchen was immense, with all of the bells and whistles. I was even a bit intimidated by some of the equipment inside it. It was nothing like the cozy little kitchen Harry and I had worked in. This place was big enough for thirty people or more to work in without getting in each other's way. All I could do was shake my head.

We turned to leave, going back the way we came, exiting through the glass insert doors. The restaurant had been pushed forward a few feet from the beach, making it feel as if it had been plopped down right on the edge of the ocean. I slipped off my shoes and dug my toes into the water and sand.

"Do you like it?" Joanna asked shyly.

"Oh, yes. I love it. Unfortunately, I won't be spending as much time here as I want. I'll be traveling a lot on the circuit."

"I know, but you love it, don't you?"

"Yes. Almost as much as I love you. If I asked you to travel with me sometimes, would you consider it?"

"If you ask me, I'll consider it." She was such a terrible tease, but I loved it.

"Then, I'm asking. Would you like to travel with me, Jo?"

"Yeah, I would."

CHAPTER TWENTY-SIX

Word of my return to competitive surfing spread even quicker than news of the new restaurant being built, and soon, my phone was ringing off the hook with calls from industry media, agents, and sponsors.

It was a rush, that feeling of being in demand again, but it was also a reminder that while the spotlight was back on me, this time, things were going to be different because I was different. With Josh, Sean, and Colin off the circuit, young guys like Jordan and I had a chance to make it big, especially having been their protégés.

I was halfway through a protein shake when Chris Bryant, my new assistant, sent me my schedule for the next month. Chris was a pro, formerly with one of the biggest talent management agencies, and he'd jumped in without missing a beat, handling all the moving parts I didn't even realize were there. Meetings, calls, sponsorship pitches—it was a whole new world, and Chris navigated it like he'd been born to do this.

"You've got a call with Element Surfboards at 10 a.m. and then a photo shoot with *Wave Riders* magazine at 2 p.m.," Chris said, reading from his tablet as he sat across from me at the café. "Also, Riptide Energy wants to lock down a deal before the end of the week. They're throwing in a huge bonus if you agree to feature them prominently on your board."

I nodded, trying to keep up. "Sounds good, but do we have any time blocked out for training?"

Chris looked up, arching an eyebrow. "Barely, but we'll make it work. You've got an hour tomorrow morning, and then we can squeeze in another session after the *Wave Riders* shoot."

Anxiety bubbled up inside me. Everything felt like it was moving at warp speed. The meetings, the deals, the constant demands on my time—it was like being pulled in a thousand different directions. And then there was The Breakwater, my other big commitment. I glanced at my phone, checking the messages from Joanna and Harry about the latest construction updates. Steel beams were going up, the windows were being installed— it was really happening. The Breakwater was coming to life.

But as excited as I was, I couldn't ignore the nagging guilt. My attention was divided, and I felt like I was letting everyone down just a little bit. I didn't want to mess this up, not for Harry, not for Joanna, and not for myself.

"Ever feel like you're juggling too much?" I asked Chris, trying to sound casual. "Like, how did you handle this when you were with the agency?"

Chris leaned back, thoughtful for a moment. "You're always going to feel stretched, Quinn. But the key is figuring out what's most important at the moment. I used to work with guys who were at the top of their game—endorsements, interviews, the whole nine yards. But only a few really set aside time in their schedules to decompress, to ground themselves. For them, it was their families, hobbies, or side interests. You won't burn out as fast if you do it. You have family, and you have The Breakwater."

His words struck a chord. I realized that, in the chaos of getting back into the game, I'd have to cherish and celebrate the moments that made it all worth it—the quiet mornings on the water, the satisfaction of watching The Breakwater take shape. Spending time with Joanna and Harry. I'll need to find balance in all of those moments.

Just then, my phone buzzed with a notification—a sponsorship pitch from a wetsuit company I'd never heard of. Another demand for my attention. I sighed, feeling the weight of it all pressing down on me.

Chris noticed and gave me a reassuring nod. "We'll get through this, Quinn. You're not in this alone."

I nodded, grateful for his presence. "Thanks, Chris. Seriously. I think I'd be lost without your help."

He smirked. "You're doing great. Just remember, we are not going to say yes to everything. We'll just focus on what feels right to you and your goals."

That advice stayed with me after we wrapped up our meeting. I had a lot on my plate, but I wasn't going to let that keep me from enjoying this moment, from appreciating how far I'd come. I was back on the circuit, and The Breakwater was almost ready to open its doors. Everything was happening at once, but I was determined to find a way to make it all work.

As Chris and I walked out of the café, a few fans recognized me and asked for autographs and selfies. I obliged, feeling the buzz of celebrity status. It was flattering, sure, but it also reminded me that every choice I made now mattered.

We headed back to the site, and as I looked at the gleaming structure of The Breakwater, a sense of calm washed over me. I was juggling a lot, but this—this place—was my anchor. I was also excited to be carving out my own path on the water.

CHAPTER TWENTY-SEVEN

I'd spent the night restless and wide awake, nervously hoping everything would go according to plan.

Sleep had eluded me, even though I'd spent a grueling ten days on the circuit, winning in nice-size purses in Montañita and Rincón and making it in the night before to be home for the grand opening. My mind raced with a mix of excitement and nerves. Who knew life was leading me down this path.

Knowing I wouldn't get any sleep, I'd eased out of bed, trying not to wake Joanna. She looked so peaceful, and for a moment, I just watched her, feeling a deep sense of gratitude that she was part of this journey. But as I stood there, the weight of the upcoming day pressed on me. What if everything wasn't enough? What if the changes we'd made didn't live up to everyone's expectations? My mind replayed every decision, every detail we'd poured into this place.

I slipped out of the bedroom and the apartment over the garage that once stood behind the old building that was no longer. The courtyard between the garage and the old building still existed, but it had also received a makeover, providing outdoor space we could use for our own purposes or terrace dining. I headed down to the beach, hoping the sound of the waves might calm me. Harry was due back today, and I was excited for him to see his dream made real. He thought he was coming back to see to the final touches, but he would be coming home to the grand opening. We'd invited all of his friends and customers to christen the restaurant with us tonight as a surprise for him.

I stood with my feet in the sand, the backwash rolling up over my ankles and looked back at the beautiful, single-story Spanish-style building sitting at the edge of the sand. The plate glass windows and terracotta clay tile roof gleamed in the soft predawn light. It was everything I had envisioned and more. I took it all in, feeling a swell of pride. I had so much to be grateful for.

That evening, we dressed in our party finery. Joanna looked gorgeous in a bronze chiffon dress that reflected the light like a fiery sunset while I put on a pair of linen slacks and button-down, my sleeves folded back and pushed up on my forearms and the collar open. It was as dressy as I was willing to get, but I had to admit, I looked rather stylish.

There were three dining rooms in the restaurant, and each room could open up to the others, making the space completely open, and it seemed filled to capacity. It seemed like every soul Harry and Joanna knew in San Nobel had been invited. Customers, friends and vendors that Harry knew from his days in the Shack, and family, friends and coworkers of Joanna from the bank. The place buzzed with energy, the sounds of laughter and conversation blending with the gentle crash of the waves coming through the open accordion-style doors. I stood at the entrance, taking it all in—the warm glow of the lights, the murmur of the ocean, the happy faces of our friends and customers. This was what I'd hoped for, seeing Harry and Joanna happy. I'd watched Joanna moving through the crowd, chatting and sharing stories, practically radiant as the hostess of the evening. Seeing how she interacted with everyone, I realized just how much of a cornerstone she had become—not just in this place but in my life. We had built something beautiful together, not just in wood and paint, but a shared dream and maybe even love.

As I caught glimpses of her flitting in and out of the crowd, my thoughts drifted to how far I'd come in less than a year. I was back on the surfing circuit, earning enough money to not only replace what we'd spent on the renovations but money to put away for the future. Josh had come through for me, opening doors I never thought would be open, and sponsorship and endorsement offers were piling up. I'd been dubbed the *Protégé* by one of the magazines that had been obsessed with Josh, Sean, and the team back before the accident, back when we were on top, and the name had stuck. According to the lore that was building around me, I'd supposedly inherited the tides, taking over from Josh, Sean, and Colin. I was a rising star in the surfing world, burning as bright as a supernova, a name that was on the tip of everyone's tongue. So different than when I'd landed in San Nobel in the back of a rideshare eleven months ago, a dejected, depressed wreck, willing to surrender myself, my life to the ocean. I chuckled self-deprecatingly. How fortunate the ocean didn't want me or my life.

"Quinn!" Harry's voice brought me back to the moment. He was over at the bar, his eyes sparkling with pride as he surveyed the room. I hurried over to him, clapping him on the back, and he handed me a shot of bourbon. We clinked glasses and tossed the drink back in a toast.

"We did it, Harry," I said, unable to keep the joy out of my voice. "Look at this place—it's incredible."

Harry chuckled, his eyes twinkling with pride. "You and Joanna done good, Kid. This place... it's something special now."

I beamed, my heart swelling with the pride of our shared accomplishment. "We all did this, Harry. You, me, Joanna—this is as much your legacy as it is mine or Joanna's. You were the rock we built upon."

Harry nodded, a moment of understanding passing between us. The Breakwater was a new chapter in a life well-lived, and for me, it was a home I could always come back to, no matter where the waves might take me.

"What about the décor in the back, leading to the offices?" Harry asked, waving his hand. "That was your idea?"

"Yeah. I wanted a place for all of the things I've collected over the years. Some of it belonged to a dear friend of mine."

"You should've made a space to put them on display. They're phenomenal," Harry praised me as we walked back to look at them together. The space that Joanna had named The Wall of Fame was a long and extra-wide corridor with three large offices opening off of it. The walls we decorated with my special surfboards, years of collected memorabilia, and carefully chosen decorations. Some of Colin's gear, which Sean had given me after the accident that had taken him from us, were displayed inside glass cases, alongside posters, autographed pictures, and magazine covers featuring my teammates; most showed us hamming it up on the beaches for the crowd. Posters from surfing events around the world adorned the walls, a testament to the life I'd lived and the one I was still building. It had all come together, a part of my past but also a part of my future in this special place.

"I think it's perfect," he said, beaming at me.

"Yeah, it is perfect." I agreed, but I wished my old teammates, my brothers, had been here to see it and share this moment with me. They were still family, and I hoped they knew that. I'd done my part, calling and inviting them all, but they'd each had a prior engagement. Even Jordan had to decline as he was competing in J'Bay, South Africa. I know I was being sentimental and maybe even a little jealous, though I could hardly expect any one of them to be just sitting around, excited to get a party invite from me. They had their own lives, their own paths. But a part of me wished they could've spent one evening with me. I followed Harry back out into the noisy main room, intent on finding Joanna and playing my part as the host with the most. Looking around for her, I heard a familiar voice cut through the crowd.

"Quinn, Dude. What's a guy gotta do to get a drink around

here?" said that voice I'd know anywhere.

I turned around, and there they were—Marc and Vince, Jordan, Grayson, Joey, and Lloyd—all grinning like they'd just pulled off the best prank ever. My heart skipped a beat as I processed the sight of them, my brothers, standing right in front of me.

"You guys… What the hell!" I laughed, pulling Jordan into a big bear hug, followed by the rest of the crew. "What are you doing here?"

Jordan smirked, slapping my back. "We couldn't let you have all the fun, man. And we come bearing gifts."

They each handed me something—a framed photo of our first win together, an old trophy from a competition that seemed like a lifetime ago, Colin's favorite cap that Joey had been given. I stared at the items in my hands, feeling the weight of the memories they carried.

"These are—" My voice cracked, and I cleared my throat, fighting back the wave of emotion. "You guys didn't have to do this."

Grayson, usually the stoic one, patted my shoulder. "Yeah, we did. It's not about having to. It's about showing up for our brother."

"Thank you," I said, my voice thick. "This means more than you know. Come on, let me show you my infamous Wall of Fame."

I led them down the corridor, my footsteps echoing slightly off the polished floors. The lighting was soft, casting a warm glow that highlighted every piece on the walls—the surfboards, the photos, the memorabilia, all the little things that had defined our journey together. I could feel their eyes scanning the walls, taking it all in, and I watched as their expressions shifted from curiosity to something deeper. Jordan stopped in front of the photo of our first win, his fingers brushing the frame as if to make sure it was real. "Man, I remember this day like it was yesterday. That was the first time I ever felt like we really had something, you know? Like we weren't just kids out there, but a team."

Grayson let out a low whistle, his eyes lingering on Colin's old surfboard, mounted just above eye level. "I don't even have the words. It's like you've put our whole story right here on these walls."

Marc traced a finger along the edge of a faded competition poster, one of our early matches where we were still figuring each other out. "This is everything, Quinn. Every win, every wipe-out. Every damn thing we went through is right here."

I watched them as they moved down the wall, each stopping at different points, their hands reaching out to touch pieces of our past. The board that Colin had ridden in his last competition, Joey's sun-faded rash guard from the Florida Pro, the trophy from that impossible comeback in Malibu. Each item told a story, a chapter of the life we had built together, and seeing them all here, together, felt like the ultimate homecoming.

"This wall is sick, Quinn," Lloyd said, his voice thick with emotion. "It's ours. It's like you made a place for all of us, all of it—everything we've been through, everything we are. You've honored Colin, Josh and Sean in a way none of us could have done alone."

I nodded, my throat tight as I tried to hold back the tears. "You guys were my family when I had nothing else. I wouldn't have been here at this point in my life without you guys."

Jordan looked around, his eyes shimmering. "It's perfect, Q. You've made sure none of us will ever be forgotten."

"Well, now you have a few more mementos to add to your infamous wall." I know I was grinning like a deranged person as I stood there looking at each of them. Their faces were full of pride and something deeper—love, maybe, the kind that doesn't need to be spoken aloud, but I felt full to bursting.

"Okay, so, seriously," Jeff started, giving me a one-arm hug and then a punch to my bicep, which almost made me drop everything. "I really do want that drink, and I saw some pretty ladies I'd rather be chatting up than you hard legs."

"Yeah, okay," I responded, getting a hold of my emotions. "Go on back out and get yourselves something to drink while I put these in the office. Then we can find something to eat, and you can chat up the pretty ladies all night."

The guys headed back out to the party and presumably over to the bar, and I took the gifts they'd given me to my office. However, Joanna surprised me when she tapped on the open office door, her voice gentle yet insistent. "Quinn, there's someone here who's been waiting to see you."

I turned, half expecting another one of the old crew, but the sight that met my eyes left me speechless. Joanna stood next to a tiny, frail little woman with silver-streaked hair, wearing a soft, uncertain smile—my mother. I blinked, stunned, as the room seemed to tilt for a moment.

"Momma?" The word caught in my throat. I hadn't seen her in what felt like forever, and it took me a second to believe she was really here. "What… What are you doing here?"

She stepped forward, her eyes brimming with tears. "I wouldn't miss this for the world, Quinn. I'm so proud of you."

My breath hitched. She looked the same but different—older, frailer, but also stronger. And softer, too. And seeing her here, at the Breakwater, in the middle of this new life I'd built, was almost too much. All the memories of us together—the good ones, the hard ones—rushed back, filling the space between us.

I glanced at Joanna, and she smiled at me and took the gifts I was about to drop again. I gave her a quick kiss before she moved away, then I moved toward my mom, and she pulled me into a tight embrace, her arms wrapping around me like she was holding on for dear life. I closed my eyes, letting the familiarity of her touch wash over me, grounding me in a way I hadn't realized I needed. Finally, I squeezed her in my arms until she squeaked.

"I'm sorry I didn't come to see you sooner," she whispered, her voice trembling. "I wanted to come see you right after Christmas. I saw you were here from the return address on your gift."

I pulled back, looking at her through the haze of emotion. "I'm glad you're here right now. I've missed you. Where's Dad? Did he come too?"

She shook her head and wiped a tear from her cheek, but her smile widened. "No, and that's okay. He'll have no one to blame but himself. But you…you've come a long way, Quinn. You've built something beautiful here. I always knew you would do something with your life. You were always smart, so strong-willed."

"I had a little help and a lot of inspiration," I said smiling at Joanna, having returned from the back office. I reached out for her and clasped her hand in mine. My mom reached out, squeezing Joanna's arm with a grateful smile. "Thank you for bringing us back together."

Joanna nodded, tears glistening in her eyes. "He deserves to have everyone who loves him here with him." I squeezed Mom again and leaned over to give Joanna a kiss on the cheek. Now everything was alright in the world.

CHAPTER
TWENTY-EIGHT

The next morning, the beach was bathed in the soft, early light of dawn, the sun just beginning to lift above the horizon.

The waves were small but perfect, rolling in gently like they were welcoming us back. We sat in the cool sand, the five of us, the tips of our boards dug into the sand beside us. None of us were in any rush to paddle out. The guys were leaving today and though it saddened me that they were dispersing to parts all over the world, my heart was full knowing we'd reconnected with one another.

Jordan broke the quiet, his voice carrying that familiar mix of excitement and nostalgia. "Feels like old times. Just us and the ocean. No pressure, no crowds, just…this."

I nodded, soaking in the moment. "Yeah, but it feels different, doesn't it? I feel different, I guess. We're not those kids anymore."

Grayson laughed, a deep, throaty sound that echoed over the water. "Nah, man. We've seen too much and lost too much. But that's why things matter now, more than ever. It's like that song, you know? We're still standing."

Joey looked out at the waves, a wistful smile on his face. "Remember how we used to watch Josh, Sean, and Colin? How we'd be sitting like this on the beach, dreaming about the day we'd be out there, too? I never thought it would happen like this, but maybe it was our destiny."

Jordan nodded, the weight of our shared history reflected in his eyes. "I don't know about destiny and all that, but they taught us everything. Not just about surfing but about life. How to push through, how to keep going even when it felt impossible. We owe them everything for what they gave us."

Lloyd spoke up, his voice quieter but no less sure. "We're their legacy now. They're gone, but their story isn't over. Not if we keep it alive."

I felt a lump in my throat as I looked around at my brothers. We were all battered in different ways, carrying scars both visible and hidden. But standing here, I realized we'd become exactly what we'd once idolized. Not perfect, but determined. Not invincible, but unbreakable.

"We've earned this," I said, feeling the truth of it settle in my chest. "We've put in the work and paid our dues. And now it's our turn. We're not just filling their shoes—we'll be making our own path."

Jordan grinned, his confidence radiating out like sunlight. "Hell yeah. It is our time. We're gonna take every wave, every title, and make our mark. We're not the next Josh, Sean, and Colin. We're the first of our names. And we're gonna be legends."

We stood there for a moment, the gravity of what we were

saying hanging in the air between us. It felt right. We'll be the new guard, the ones who were going to step up and carry on where they left off."

Grayson clapped me on the shoulder, his grip firm. "We've got your back. Always."

The ocean called to us then, a soft roar that echoed the promise of endless possibilities. We picked up our boards, and for a moment, I ran my hand over the familiar nicks and scratches, the battle scars of countless waves, each one a piece of our story. I grinned at Jordan, and he grinned back, and we took off and sprinted toward the water.

We all paddled out, side by side, catching the first wave of the day with the same joy we'd felt as kids. The water lifted us, cradling us in its embrace, and for a few perfect moments, it was like nothing had changed, and everything had changed all at once. As I rode that wave, feeling the rush of the wind and the spray of the sea, I knew we were ready. The past was behind us, and the future—our future—was wide open. We were no longer chasing someone else's dream. This was our time, our story. The sun broke over the horizon, casting our shadows long and triumphant against the water. Together, we carved our path into the morning, each turn and twist a promise of what was to come. We were just getting started.

Acknowledgments

Thank you for taking this journey with me. Whether you've been with me from the beginning with Josh and Sean in Shifting Tides, or joined along the way, meeting them in Sean's story, Wild Tides, or you're meeting Quinn, Jordan, and the rest of the crew for the first time here in Inherit The Tides, I am deeply grateful for your support and enthusiasm. Writing this trilogy has been a labor of love, filled with highs and lows, much like the waves our characters ride.

From the first page of the first book to the final words of this third and final installment, you've stayed with me through every twist, turn, heartbreak, and triumph. Your commitment to these characters and their stories means more than I can express.

I hope these books have given you moments of escape, of reflection, of excitement, and maybe even inspiration. It's been a privilege to share this world with you, and I couldn't have done it without the encouragement and support of readers like you.

Thank you for being part of this adventure. Here's to chasing waves, dreams, and everything in between.

With gratitude,

E V McMillan